AN AVALON HISTORICAL ROMANCE

SHERIFF'S CHOICE
Jane McBride Choate

Colorado Springs, a booming town in a new state, has come a long way. It boasts a school, a post office, and even a library. But rustling is stripping local ranchers of their livelihoods. The town council has brought Ford McKinnon, a sheriff with a reputation of a fast gun and a cool hand, to put an end to it.

Ford McKinnon has never belonged—not to a place, not to a woman, not even to himself, only to the job.

Cady Armstrong, on the contrary, belongs to Colorado Springs. Owner and editor of the *Colorado Springs Gazette*, she reports the news, writes the editorials, and prints the paper. The daughter of the town's former sheriff, Cady has a special interest in watching how the new sheriff handles himself, and she isn't impressed.

Ford and Cady have nothing in common, except a desire for the truth. But what they discover might divide them forever.

Other books by Jane McBride Choate:

Design to Deceive
Sweet Lies and Rainbow Skies
Mustang Summer
All That I Ask
Match Made in Heaven
Think of Me
Convincing David
Heartsong Lullaby
Never Too Late for Christmas
Mile-High Love
Cheyenne's Warrior Rainbow
Desert Paintbox
Wolf's Eye
Star Crossed

SHERIFF'S
CHOICE

•

Jane McBride Choate

AVALON BOOKS
NEW YORK

Published by Thomas Bouregy & Co., Inc.
160 Madison Avenue, New York, NY 10016

Library of Congress Cataloging-in-Publication Data

Choate, Jane McBride.
    Sheriff's choice / Jane McBride Choate.
        p.   cm.
    ISBN 978-0-8034-9897-6   (acid-free paper)
    1. Colorado Springs (Colo.)—Fiction.   I. Title.

    PS3553.H575S54 2008
    813'.54—dc22   2007047384

PRINTED IN THE UNITED STATES OF AMERICA
ON ACID-FREE PAPER
BY HADDON CRAFTSMEN, BLOOMSBURG, PENNSYLVANIA

Dedicated to:
Amanda Harte, sister Avalon author and a true
friend, and Red Hatters everywhere. Remember,
normal is only a setting on the dryer.

Chapter One

Ford McKinnon had never belonged—not to a place, not to a woman, not even to himself. Only to the job.

For as long as he could remember, his work had defined him. A great deal of what he knew about himself he had learned on the job.

Hopscotching over the Southwest for the last ten years had brought him here to Colorado Springs. It was, he'd promised himself, the last stop. He'd been honing his skills until he felt ready for the job he had prepared for his whole life—to become a United States marshal.

Colorado Springs in the 1880s had come a long way. With statehood only a few years behind it, Colorado had come into its own. The Springs boasted its own school, a post office, even a library. Along with progress had come the problems that beset any growing town.

Rustling was stripping local ranchers of their livelihoods. The town council had brought in Ford to put an end to it.

Being sheriff had started as a job, one more in a string of jobs to reach his goal.

Now it was personal.

His attempts to track down the rustlers had come to nothing. The locals didn't trust him. Even his deputy was withholding judgment.

He shoved those thoughts from his mind to concentrate on what the mayor was saying.

"Well, Sheriff, what are you fixing on doing? We're being robbed blind." Mayor Gardner, hands resting on his considerable paunch, had one of the biggest spreads in the area and wasn't reluctant to use his office to push his own interests.

Ford understood the mayor well enough. The man had a bone-deep stingy streak. Word was he ran the town with the same closed fist with which he held the reins on his ranch. Ford didn't hold that against him. He had worked too long and too hard not to respect a man who held on to what was his.

He looked out over the group that had gathered in the small office. The rustlers had hit another ranch the night before. He had no clues and was no closer to finding those responsible than his predecessor had been.

The ranchers had a right to expect more from him. He had a reputation as a man who got the job done.

The job.

It had made him who he was. More, it had saved him. When he'd lost his ma, quickly followed by his pa, he'd floundered, looking for a reason to keep going. Working first as a deputy, then as a sheriff, he'd found his place. What's more, he'd discovered he was good at it.

The burly men stared at him with expressions ranging from disbelief to outright hostility. A few years ago, his temper would have had him lashing back at the accusations leveled at him. His temper had earned him more than a few broken bones and lost jobs. Older and, he hoped, wiser, he reined in his anger.

These days he preferred thinking over fighting.

If you don't get smarter, getting older is more trouble than it's worth.

His pa's words came back to him, as clear now as they had been more than twenty years ago when Ford had had more swagger than good sense. Thom McKinnon hadn't had the book learning that Ford's mother had enjoyed, but he had been smart in other ways.

His pa had taught Ford everything he knew about tracking, hunting, and surviving in the wilderness with nothing but a rifle and a canteen of water. He'd also taught Ford when to speak and when to listen.

Now was the time to listen.

Mayor Gardner shifted to fold his arms across a beefy chest. "We hired you to put an end to the rustling."

"You came highly recommended," put in another man.

" 'Highly recommended.' What does that mean?" That from Nils Jensen, the owner of the General Mercantile.

Ford leaned back, stretched his legs under the desk, and slouched just enough to give the air that Jensen's words hadn't touched a nerve. Then he leveled a gaze at each man in turn. "It means I'm still alive."

A few returned his look. The others turned away.

"Some folks are saying you haven't tried very hard." A wiry rancher shoved the town newspaper across the desk.

Ford's patience developed a dent.

Cady Armstrong. Editor and owner of the *Springs Gazette*. She had been riding him about the rustling ever since he arrived in Colorado Springs. He chalked it up to the fact that her pa had been sheriff up until three months ago, when he'd died of a heart attack.

The lady newspaper editor had been a thorn in his side ever since. Her editorials had pointed out in scathing terms his lack of progress in putting an end to the rustling.

Ford had no quarrel with her personally. She had a sharp mind and a pen to match. She didn't mind using the latter on him at every opportunity. He ignored the quick twist of annoyance as he recalled her last editorial.

What kind of man have we brought to the Springs? Does he care enough about our town to put an end to the rustling, or is the job but one more stepping-stone in his goal of becoming a United States marshal?

His irritation stemmed more from the fact that the lady had hit the nail squarely on the head than from her questioning of his abilities. He *had* taken the job as a means to an end. His goal to become a marshal had started years ago. He wouldn't apologize for it.

That didn't mean he didn't intend to serve the town and its people to the best of his ability. Giving his best, doing his best, being his best—those efforts had defined him from the moment he was sworn in as sheriff.

Still, the lady editor had a right to express her opinion. Frustration shimmered around him as he worked to make himself believe that.

He focused his annoyance into a more constructive form of energy.

Determination.

A muscle tensed in his jaw, and he turned his attention back to the men who watched him with varying degrees of skepticism. "You hired me to put an end to the rustling," he said, and frustration leaked into his voice. "I gave you my word. I intend to keep it."

The men filed out, leaving him alone with his thoughts.

In many ways, his job allowed a large margin of freedom. That was a plus. He had time to get to know the people, the rhythm of the town.

Everything about the Springs was peaceful—except for the rustling. That took him full circle, back to Cady Armstrong.

He'd barely spoken a dozen sentences to the woman since his arrival in town. He'd come away impressed by her dedication and, at the same time, irritated by her persistence in painting him as incompetent because he'd failed to capture the rustlers.

A woman running the town newspaper didn't bother him. He was enlightened enough to believe that a determined woman could do anything she set her mind to. No doubt about it, Cady was determined.

He reread the editorial. The lady had one thing right. A sheriff didn't keep his job for long when he failed to protect the townspeople.

He would make this job, this place, work.

Cady Armstrong couldn't help the spurt of pride that surged through her as the first paper slid from the press. The knowledge that she was editor of the

Springs Gazette still had the power to thrill her. Editor, copy setter, reporter, and repairman, she thought. Her hands still bore the ink stains from her last wrestling match with the huge press.

She had started with a weekly paper. Soon, she promised herself, she would have a daily one, like the one in Boston where she had apprenticed for two years. Until then, she was content. With her job, with herself.

Cady had known what she wanted to do ever since she was a child, and her father, Sam, had taken her to Denver, where she'd seen her first newspaper. The daily paper, with its columns and political cartoons, had fascinated her.

Running a newspaper had been her dream for as long as she could remember. That it had come true was largely because of Sam.

While most men regarded anything beyond reading and ciphering as wasteful, especially for a girl child, Sam had encouraged her to learn everything she could. She had girlfriends whose parents took them out of school to keep house and to tend the younger children.

Not so with Sam.

"I was never much on book learning, but you take to it right smart," he'd told her when she was only eight.

Books were scarcer than gold and twice as precious in the Colorado Territory. Sam had sent away to Denver for a dictionary for her. She remembered reverently lifting the pages, careful not to tear them.

She'd asked him how he'd paid for it, only to have him shrug off the question. Months later she'd discovered he'd sold his favorite hunting rifle to pay for the dictionary.

Sam Armstrong would never be called an astute businessman, but he'd been mother and father, friend and teacher, and everything else to her.

Thirty years ago, Colorado Springs had been a cow town, wide open, with the only law a circuit judge who came by every third month. Now there were families, a school, even a church. The arrival of the railroad had done a lot to bring the outside world to the Springs.

Mail was delivered, a town council organized— there was even talk of putting up platforms to keep the ladies' skirts from dragging in the mud and muck that were the streets.

A saloon had also opened up. Any husband who entered the establishment found an irate wife when he returned home. The town women had a grapevine that moved information faster than the drums of the Cheyenne.

Cady chuckled when she remembered the mayor's wife dragging her husband home when he'd stepped foot inside the saloon. It had taken only one woman talking to another for Mrs. Gardner to learn of her husband's visit to the saloon.

The mayor had kept his nose clean ever since.

After Cady's apprenticeship in Boston, she'd earned a job on the Denver paper. She'd made the train trip to the Springs as frequently as possible. She'd missed Sam and, much to her surprise, the town as well.

Now she was home. Sam's death had brought her back. The clutch in her heart had eased enough to allow her to remember him without the all-too-familiar pain that had crippled her for the first month after his death.

She'd packed the few belongings she'd collected while living in the city and hadn't looked back. She hadn't regretted her decision to leave Denver.

Four years ago, she couldn't wait to shake the dust of Colorado Springs from her feet. There were no secrets there, no privacy.

Hattie Marsden, the postmistress, knew who was getting mail and who wasn't. Horace Silas, president of the bank, knew who was behind in paying their bills, who had a tidy sum in savings, who couldn't buy the new plow needed for spring planting. Nils Jensen, owner of the Mercantile, knew who bought his wife a fancy parasol all the way from Denver and who purchased the most expensive yard goods when everyone knew her husband couldn't afford even the cheapest calico.

All felt compelled to share their knowledge with the rest of the town. Everything was chewed over, digested, and spit out at the open-air cafe where Doris Conway served up cherry pie and common sense with the same no-frills manner.

No one questioned the way of things.

In spite of, or maybe because everyone knew everyone else's business, the town pulled together in times of crisis and grief.

Colorado Springs was her home. That said it all. She knew these people, knew how they thought, what they believed. What's more, she genuinely liked them. When Sam died, they had enveloped her with love. Though she hadn't lived in Colorado Springs in over four years, she was still one of their own.

Small-town living, with its routine and its sameness, had cramped her when she was younger. She'd longed for the excitement and the energy, the color and the noise of the city. Now those same homely rituals gave her a sense of belonging.

Friends and neighbors enfolded her into their midst as though she'd never been gone. Some offered words of comfort over Sam, others took her into their arms and hugged her. Cakes and sympathy were served up in equal doses. She welcomed both, recognizing that the body needed nourishment while the heart grieved.

With Sam gone, the town was her family.

Seamlessly, Cady fit back into the rhythm of Colorado Springs life. Experience in the outside world had given her an appreciation for her hometown that twenty-two years of living there had failed to instill.

All her life she'd dreamed of travel, reporting about the world. Now she could appreciate the quiet pride the people took in their town, the sense of continuity. The predictability she'd once chafed under now felt right.

In the weeks following Sam's death, she had tended to the loose ends of his life. No one could accuse Sam of ambition. Content with his lot, he hadn't ventured beyond the limits of his hometown except for the occasional trip to Denver to visit Cady.

Sam had done his best to be both ma and pa to her. She had loved him for that just as she'd loved him when he hadn't succeeded. A grin tugged at her lips when she recalled his attempts to braid her hair. His big hands had struggled to make the plaits.

"It's clumsy I am," he'd said in disgust after several tries. But he'd kept at it, persisting until he'd finally succeeded in fashioning two scraggly braids.

She'd cut her hair when she was ten, saving them both the misery of the morning hair-braiding sessions. The sight of her whacked-off hair had brought tears to his eyes.

Sam had never pretended to be any good at "gal things," as he'd called them. He'd taught her other things instead.

"You've learned how to take care of yourself," Sam

had said when she was preparing to leave for Boston. "Now you're heading to the city. The rattlers there walk on two legs and more likely than not wear fancy clothes, but don't let them fool you. They're a sight more dangerous than anything you've seen here."

He had been right. The snakes she encountered in the city were more deadly than anything she'd had to face in the Springs, saying one thing but doing another. She'd learned her lessons well. Whether in the desert or the city, survival came first.

Sam hadn't understood her need to write, but he'd respected it. More, he'd respected her. When most men pulled their kids out of school before they'd reached twelve, Sam had encouraged her to stick it out.

No, she hadn't learned ambition at his knee, but he'd taught her other skills, ones that had served her in good stead over the years.

Every pot has to learn to stand on its own bottom.

She heard Sam's voice as clearly as though he stood next to her. For as long as she could remember, he had preached independence and self-reliance.

When she'd wanted a pad of paper and pencils, he'd given her a broom and told her to start sweeping out the office. He'd paid her two bits a week. Carefully, she'd saved each piece of silver, the jangle of coins in a tin cup a satisfying sound.

Hard work and thrift. Integrity and honor. They were qualities she'd learned early on.

Her mother had taken off shortly after Cady was born. It had been she and Sam for as long as she could remember. Fighting the tears burning behind her eyelids as the memories crowded her mind, she experienced a wave of nostalgia.

Even dead, Sam could evoke feelings in her that were stronger than her reaction to a lot of people she saw every day. He'd been bigger than life, with a headful of red hair only beginning to gray, a ready smile, and a wealth of common sense that had earned him the respect of everyone who knew him.

With an impatient sigh at her meanderings, she reminded herself she had a paper to get out. She cranked the huge press, smiling at the grind of gears shifting into place. It was the sound she loved best.

The lead story was the rustling, as it had been for the last several months. Rustlers had been systematically stripping the ranchers of their cattle. So far, the sheriff had turned up only dead ends.

Just as Sam had.

The article covered the most recent ranches to be hit. She'd talked to the owners, reported the losses. What she didn't have was an interview with the sheriff. Up until now, he'd steadfastly refused. It was time, she decided, that she try again.

Excitement raced through her at the idea of tracking down a real story. Sure, there were the usual funerals and church socials to cover. She treated them with the same professionalism she did the more serious pieces, but she couldn't deny the surge of energy that flowed through her or the anticipation that accompanied it at the thought of getting an inside story on the rustling.

Rustling hurt not only the ranchers but the rest of the town as well. Ranchers couldn't afford to buy supplies at the General Mercantile because their profits were down. Folks strapped for cash did not call on the doctor but tended to their own, with occasionally tragic results. Only two months ago, a rancher, faced with the decision to call the doctor or deliver his pregnant wife's baby on his own, had decided to risk it. Complications had arisen, and she'd died, along with the child.

The town veterinarian wasn't called out to tend injured animals. Last month, the Springs' only teacher had been let go because the town council couldn't afford to pay her.

The list kept growing. It was only natural that she would wonder about the man who had taken Sam's place. She tried to wrap her mind around the idea that someone else sat behind her father's desk, doing the job that had been Sam's for more than two and a half decades.

Being sheriff in a small town involved more than simply arresting those who'd broken the law. It meant being willing to bend the rules when necessary to honor the spirit of the law rather than upholding the letter of it. Most of all, it meant knowing the people and caring enough about them to do the right thing, even if it meant throwing away the book.

Could Ford McKinnon bring that to the job?

She remembered something else Sam had said. *If you have a question, go to the horse's mouth.*

Chapter Two

Ford McKinnon wasn't often taken by surprise. He didn't care for it.

So when Cady Armstrong appeared in his office, challenge in the tilt of her chin, he simply stared. Her dark blue skirt and white shirtwaist were starkly plain. Black cuffs protected her sleeves from printer's ink. Whatever he thought of her he kept to himself as he let his gaze travel over her.

His brief encounters with her thus far hadn't been enough to register the shining length of her hair or the freckles that marched across her nose. He took in the deep blue of her eyes and wondered how they'd look when they sparked with anger or mischief.

She smelled as fresh as the wildflowers that dotted

the mountainsides. As he drew it in, he decided the scent would muddle any man's mind.

She held out an ink-stained hand. "Cady Armstrong."

He took her hand, then held it. As he did, both of them went very still. Her hand, though small, was strong, like his own. Maybe that was why it seemed to fit against his like two halves of a whole. He was the first to recover, and he released her hand with something that felt like regret.

The ridges of callus on her hand told him more about her. She wasn't afraid of hard work, nor was she shy in letting others know that she labored for a living.

He skimmed his gaze over her slowly, letting his interest show. She was as tidy as a bandbox and twice as pretty. Her hair caught the glint of the sun streaming through the stingy windows, causing it to gleam like fool's gold.

Aware that she was subjecting him to the same scrutiny that he had dispensed, he let her take her time . . . and wondered what she saw.

Did she notice the scar that extended from his left temple to his jaw, a souvenir from a rowdy cowboy and a broken bottle? Did she find it repulsive?

Was that a hint of pain in her eyes? This was undoubtedly the first time she'd stepped into the jail since her pa died. Her eyes took on the sheen of unshed tears.

Politely, he looked away, giving her a chance to recover. For the span of a heartbeat he'd sensed a kindred spirit in her valiant attempt to hide the hurt. Hadn't he done the same when his mother died?

Delivering a prisoner had brought Ford to Colorado Springs several years back. He'd met Sheriff Sam Armstrong, a bear of a man with the blunt manners to match.

Armstrong hadn't talked much. He'd accepted the prisoner with a gruff thanks and a reluctant offer for Ford to bed down in the storeroom overnight. Only when he talked about his daughter had his eyes and voice softened. He was bursting with pride about Cady. *My Cady-did,* he'd called her.

Remembering Sam's rough-and-ready face, Ford decided the daughter must have gotten her looks from her mother. The determined lift of her chin, though, had enough of her pa in it to make him smile.

He admired her editorials, even when they were aimed at him. They showed a sharp wit mixed with a streak of humor.

"I guess you're wanting that interview." A look of impatience twisted his mouth, squinted his eyes.

"If it's convenient." She didn't wait for an invitation but pulled up a spare chair to his desk. Her tone made it clear that she wasn't moving until she got what she wanted.

Taking his time, he settled into his chair and squared one leg over the other. Fingers tented under his chin, he studied her face, searching for whatever it was that intrigued him.

There was a quality about her that compelled attention. Maybe it was the quiet determination in her eyes or the proud way she held herself. Or maybe it was the way a tiny furrow formed above the bridge of her nose while she waited.

Cady leaned forward, rested her elbows on his desk. "You have a reputation. I'm wondering if it's justified."

It was the second time in one day his reputation had been thrown up to him.

Turning his own chair around, he straddled it. "What I've done in the past isn't important. It's what I do now."

He said it with a quiet authority that Cady couldn't help but respect.

Instinct had her wanting to believe him, yet she couldn't deny his lack of progress in putting an end to the rustling.

He wasn't handsome, not in a conventional sense. His face was too angular for that, with hard planes and hollows thrown into sharp relief. Brown hair was tied at his neck with a leather thong, while long lashes shadowed eyes so dark, they were almost black.

She whipped out the small notebook she carried with her. "Give me something I can print. Folks need to know you're doing something. They're scared."

"They have a right to be. The whole town depends upon ranching."

She nodded her approval at his understanding. He understood the cycle of ranching and commerce. Those who didn't ranch sold goods to those who did.

"Why haven't you made more progress in identifying the rustlers?"

"Maybe for the same reason your pa didn't." His voice was flat, his gaze steady.

With an effort, she held on to her temper. She'd heard the criticism that Sam had been too old, too feeble, to do the job.

Ford reached out a hand, then dropped it at her glare. "Look, I'm sorry. I shouldn't have said that. Your pa was a good man. I'm sure he did his best to track down the rustlers. And that's what I'm doing. My best."

She recognized the sincerity in his voice. The man had a point. She couldn't fault him for speaking the truth. "What are you planning to do?"

"Wait them out. They're wily enough to lay low for a while and then strike again when we've let down our guard."

"In other words, nothing." She could barely keep the disappointment from her voice.

Patience had never been one of her virtues. Sam had called her on that more than once.

A man who tries to put on his pants both legs at a

time ends up tripping himself. A reluctant smile broke through her frown.

She watched as the sheriff's jaw tightened, and she resisted the urge to squirm under the palpable irritation he directed her way.

"I heard Colorado Springs was a friendly town. Looks like I was wrong."

She flushed. "It is."

His raised eyebrows told her what he thought about that.

She had judged him for no other reason than that he'd stepped into Sam's job. Her cheeks burned with shame at the unfairness of it.

She wanted to apologize, to tell him that wasn't who she was. Ever since Sam's death, though, she didn't know who she was. Sam had been the one constant in her life. Without him, she was floundering. She kept reaching for something, someone, to hold on to and knew that, for the first time in her life, she was totally alone.

Her pain over Sam's death was still too raw. She wouldn't have liked *anyone* who took his place. It didn't help that McKinnon was an outsider.

"You got a problem with me, how about telling me before you start writing about it?" He paused, his jaw muscles bunching.

He was right. She had attacked him without knowing the facts. A beginner's mistake. She felt a wash of color crawl up her neck.

To her surprise, she dropped her resentment and found herself nodding in grudging agreement. At the same time, the anger dissolved out of her posture. "You're right. I didn't want to give you a chance."

He looked surprised. Then his lips curved into a smile. "You loved your pa. No one can fill his shoes. I'm just trying to do the job the best way I know how."

The simple words touched her in a way no fancy promises could have. "I believe you," she said, and she found that she meant it.

"I'm sorry about your pa," the sheriff said with simple sympathy. "It hurts to lose family."

She blinked back tears. She couldn't say why, of all the words of sympathy she had received, these few from a man she barely knew touched her as they did. "Thank you," she said, and she cleared the huskiness from her voice, annoyed with herself for feeling vulnerable.

Ford turned his gaze away, an obvious attempt to give her a chance to pull herself together.

She reminded herself she had a job to do. "You need more deputies." The surrounding area covered a thousand square miles. One man couldn't cover the entire area. She knew that Robb Turner, the deputy sheriff, was eager to learn, but he was also young and inexperienced.

Ford's lips quirked in a reluctant smile. "The mayor's so cheap, he'd steal the bark off a dog."

Her smile sneaked up on her and spread across her

face before she realized it was there. The sheriff had described the mayor perfectly. "I wouldn't be surprised if he still has the first nickel he ever made."

"And penny."

That tickled a laugh out of her. Her breath slid down her throat as one side of his mouth turned up in a crooked grin, the one that made his dark, almost black eyes crinkle at the corners.

It surprised her that he could make her laugh. His grin was different from his smile, she noticed. The smile was slow, while the grin was a flash.

Both were appealing. Just like the man himself.

The laughter died, along with the moment of accord.

"Do you have a plan? Other than waiting out the rustlers?"

"Yeah. I've got a plan."

"Care to share it?"

"And have you publish it in that paper of yours and alert whoever's behind the rustling?" He shook his head. "I don't think so."

"Give me some credit. I wasn't going to print it."

"Weren't you?"

"Why should I?"

"Maybe to make me look foolish." His words sliced too close to home.

That was twice he'd made her feel ashamed. She didn't much like the feeling. "I want the rustling stopped as much as everyone else does."

"Good. Then stop riding me in those editorials of yours, and let me do my job. There's another reason I'm playing my cards close to the vest. I don't think the rustlers are strangers."

"You think the rustler might be someone we know?" Cady couldn't bring herself to think that. These people were her friends, her family.

Ford nodded. " 'Fraid so. I've asked around. There haven't been any strangers in town."

"If it's someone we know," she said slowly, "then why haven't we noticed? That kind of money is bound to attract attention." No one in town had much money, unless one of the ranch hands flashed some cash after a win at poker.

"Maybe he's smart enough to keep it to himself."

His response had her rethinking the situation. She shifted her gaze to take in the rest of the room and settled upon the shelves that lined the back wall. The smell of new wood, the fresh edges of it, told her that the shelves were a recent addition.

Her eyes widened when she took in the books that marched across the simple pine planks. Keats, Shakespeare, Byron. Her fingers itched to touch those leather-bound treasures. She had her own collection of books, but they were not as splendid as these.

Regardless of the condition, each of her volumes was a gem that she prized above all other possessions. Books were a passport to knowledge, to other nations, to other people. And, ultimately, to herself.

He followed her gaze. "What's wrong? Are you surprised that I read poetry? Or that I read at all?"

"The books," she said, her voice hushed in reverence. "We don't usually see ones so fine here."

Indeed, the last time she'd seen so many books was when she was in Boston, and then they had been in the library, carefully guarded by a prune-faced woman who had handed Cady a white cloth with which to wipe her hands before she was allowed to so much as touch one of the prized volumes.

"I like your motto," he said unexpectedly. " 'The pen is mightier than the sword.' "

A man who read Keats and quoted Shakespeare. Most of the men in town hadn't heard of either, much less knew the difference.

Another side to the new sheriff. She'd never have guessed he read Twain or the English classics. There were layers to this man that intrigued her as much as did the quiet authority that cloaked him like a mantle. She wondered what else lay behind the badge he wore so easily.

It didn't matter, of course. She wasn't interested in Ford McKinnon, the man, just as he wasn't interested in her beyond her editorials.

Why did the admission cause her a pang of regret?

She looked at the badge that had been her father's for more than a quarter of a century.

Throughout the interview, he'd watched her with clear, wary eyes. Now he stood. He was long of leg and rangy of body and every bit as attractive at close quarters as he was at a distance.

His smile came in a quick, hard curve. "You're not making my job any easier."

Now it was her time to smile. "No. I'm not."

"Maybe you'll see that I'm not the enemy."

"I never said you were."

"But you think it. I come along, a stranger, and take your pa's job, a job he's held for over a quarter of a century. That'd put anybody's back up."

That he understood her so completely startled her. How did she answer such simple empathy? "I might have been a little hard on you," she allowed reluctantly.

"Just a little."

He stuck out his hand, and, after a moment's hesitation, she took it.

His hand swallowed hers, drawing her attention to the sheer size of the man. Accustomed to big men, she still found him overwhelming.

"Truce?" Her mouth relaxed into a smile.

"Truce."

She stared at their linked hands, surprised by the feelings that flowed through her. The sight of her fingers cradled in his made her feel precious and fragile, a rare experience for a woman who prided herself on being as strong and as tough as any man.

She stood. When his dark eyes swept the length of

her, she felt as though summer lightning had suddenly struck her.

Tension, real and tangible, seemed to fill the air. At the same time, she felt curiously breathless. She inhaled deeply, needing to clear her mind. Suddenly she was aware of every pore, every nerve. Each seemed to draw taut under his unwavering stare.

The cock of his chin, the thumbs hooked in his belt, the way his weight was balanced on the balls of his feet made her think of a mountain lion ready to pounce upon unsuspecting prey.

Chapter Three

Ford wrapped his hands around a mug of coffee. There was no reason for Cady Armstrong to still be on his mind. That one moment of connection between them had been a quirk. His smile flickered as he recalled her straight-from-the-hip questions that hadn't bothered with politeness.

He didn't make the mistake of underestimating her. He'd met too many women who had grit and courage to spare; women who had fought alongside their men. And, in some cases, had died.

He tilted his chair back, annoyed that the scent of ink and sunshine still lingered in the air. He'd felt himself responding to it, to her.

It was ridiculous that her image kept chasing through his thoughts, for him to remember exactly the way her hand had felt inside his own, the way her eyes had gone from wary to startled, then softly warm.

Small-town life had a rhythm. Whenever anything—or anyone—added a new beat, everyone felt it. Sam Armstrong's daughter was definitely a new beat.

His interest in her was another.

His reaction to her was not a simple one, not even one that made sense.

She was Sam's daughter all right, he thought with more than a trace of admiration. Straight as an arrow and all business. Though she didn't favor the lawman in looks, she had the same chin, set in determination when she wanted something, and the same streak of integrity.

Ford had spent years learning to make swift but accurate judgments of others. His job, his very life, had depended on that ability.

He had faced drunken cowboys, men who would shoot another over a thirty-dollar poker game, and the meanest of outlaws. After thirty minutes with Cady Armstrong, he was tied up in knots like a schoolboy mooning over his first girl.

It was all right to recall the color of her hair—it was a gleaming blend of russet and gold he wouldn't soon forget—but he shouldn't know the color of her eyes. You had to be paying attention to notice eyes.

Cady's eyes reminded him of the Colorado sky at

midday—startling, blindingly blue. They had a way of seeing through him and making him aware he didn't measure up.

It wasn't surprising she should feel that way. Her father had been sheriff for twenty-five years. He'd given his life to the town, dying of a heart attack when he was barely fifty.

No man could fill his shoes, least of all in his daughter's eyes. Ford wondered why he should find the thought so depressing.

She had challenged him at every level and annoyed him beyond what was reasonable. He had yet to figure out why.

How had she managed to invade his mind so completely when he had spoken less than a dozen sentences to her? He had met women equally as attractive but never such a compelling one, and never had one made such an impact on him as had this one.

Outspoken and blunt, she wasn't the type of woman he was normally attracted to. So why was her image, the scent of her, stuck in his mind?

The pretty reporter had gotten under his skin.

Darned if the lady wasn't appealing, with her sassy mouth and sharp insights. Her size was misleading. He wouldn't be surprised if it caused others to underestimate her. He wouldn't make that mistake.

His encounter with Cady Armstrong was still gnawing at him. His ego wasn't so fragile that he couldn't take her riding him in her editorials. What was eating at him was his reaction to her. When she'd offered him her hand, he'd felt something. Her touch had set off sparks that still had him reeling.

He wanted to chalk it up to shock, but he knew it was more basic than that. He was attracted to her. Heck, *attraction* didn't begin to describe what he'd felt when his hand closed around hers.

He shook his head, impatient with his musings. He had a job to do, and he wasn't likely to find the answers staring out the window to the dusty street beyond. With the profit margin in ranching as narrow as it was, cattlemen couldn't afford major losses.

Thoughts of the rustling stirred uneasy speculation within him. Sam Armstrong had been a tough, experienced lawman. Why hadn't he found one clue to the rustlers' identity in the past eighteen months?

It didn't add up.

Ford liked the order and predictability of patterns. Look for the pattern, and you'll discover the whole. One part of the pattern was missing.

He filed his speculations away and concentrated on what he did know. The rustlers had worked their way from one end of the county to the other.

Maybe he was approaching this from the wrong angle. Instead of worrying over where the rustlers had already hit, maybe he ought to be looking for where they would strike next.

He unfolded his legs from behind the desk, stood, and strapped on his gun. He'd used his gun more times than he wanted to remember, though fewer than his reputation reported. Contrary to what others believed, he didn't draw his gun unless there was no alternative.

A gun, even a fast gun, didn't make a man. It had taken him years to understand that, more to accept it.

He felt more a man today than he had a dozen years ago when he'd done his best to earn a reputation as a fast gun. He'd worked hard to rid himself of that same reputation. Character, not a fast trigger finger, made the man.

"In you go," Robb said as he shoved two men into the office. "Howie here picked a fight with Jeb Lassiter over at Flynn's place," he explained.

Ford looked up in annoyance. He'd used up his store of patience for the day. And then some. "Have them empty their pockets, and then toss them into a cell."

"Heck, Sheriff, you aren't going to lock us up for a little roughhousing, are ya?" Lassiter whined.

"Yeah," Howie Marlow seconded. "We was just having a little fun."

"Your 'fun's' gonna cost Flynn over fifty dollars in damages," Robb said.

Ford whistled. Fifty dollars represented a month's profit for the saloon. Maybe two.

The two men grumbled but offered no further protests as the deputy led them to the cells.

"What was that all about?" Ford asked when Robb returned.

"Howie called Jeb a horse's . . ."

Ford kept his smile under wraps.

"Then Jeb said Howie wouldn't know one end of a horse from the other," Robb said, his voice developing a noticeable drawl as he warmed to his story.

The smile wouldn't stay hidden. "I get the picture."

"Funny thing." Robb rubbed the back of his neck. "Jeb and Howie were arguing about something. First time I've ever seen Howie mad enough to even raise his voice, much less take a swing at someone."

"Too much to drink?"

Robb looked unconvinced. "Maybe."

Ford filed away that bit of information for later. Robb was a homegrown boy who knew the town and its citizens. More than once he'd filled in Ford on a situation, preventing Ford from jumping in with both feet before knowing the facts.

Knowledge is power. His ma had drummed those words into his head when Ford could scarcely reach her knee as she read to him from one of her books.

He recalled her words as she'd told him how she'd left behind everything else, save for the clothes on her back, to make room for her scores of books when she'd followed Ford's father west. Her soft voice had turned husky in the telling.

Ford traveled light, never accumulating much of

anything, but the books went where he did. He read late at night, memorizing passages from the great writers whose words remained as powerful today as they were hundreds of years ago.

Not many people knew of his passion for books. It wasn't something he advertised. In a town where most of the men couldn't write their own names, reading and writing came far down on the list of valuable skills.

Robb shuffled from one foot to the other, a sure sign that he had something to get off his chest.

"Spit it out," Ford invited.

"People are talking," Rob said reluctantly.

"What are they saying?"

"That you've lost your nerve," the deputy answered. "That you're scared and that's why you won't go after the rustlers."

Ford wasn't surprised. Hadn't the mayor and his minions said almost the same thing? "What do you think?"

"I think you're the best there is—next to Sam, that is." The obvious sincerity in Robb's voice warmed Ford. But Robb was more boy than man and susceptible to being impressed by a reputation.

"Thanks for that."

"You're welcome. Only, Sheriff, what *are* you doing to stop the rustling?"

So, the boy wasn't all that impressed, Ford thought.

Well, he hadn't done anything to impress anyone lately. "Not enough."

He scribbled out a message, then handed Robb some coins. "Take this to the telegraph office. Have Joe send it to every sheriff in the state."

Robb nodded. "Sure thing, Sheriff."

Ford went over the notes he'd made, still looking for the pattern. He knew it was there; he could feel it. He just couldn't see it.

By evening he was frustrated with his lack of progress. He made his final rounds of the nearly sleeping town, satisfied that the storefronts were locked tight. He was working his way to the *Gazette* when he heard the commotion.

He found Cady with an arm around Emilie Browne outside the doctor's office. Emilie had a black eye, the kind that came when a man's fist met flesh.

Cady lifted a grim gaze to his. "The doc's out on a call," she said.

"What happened?" he asked, but he was afraid he already knew.

Emilie put a hand to her eye. "It's nothing. . . . I fell and thought maybe I could get the doc to look at my eye."

Ford let his gaze take in the woman, her eye nearly swollen shut. He didn't think Emilie had fallen or that the bruises that smudged her neck and collarbone were the result of a fall. Cal Browne had a reputation for beating his wife whenever he'd had too much to drink.

He didn't see any need for pretending that Emilie's pathetic lie had fooled him. "You didn't get that black eye from a fall."

Emilie bit back a sob. "Cal promised he'd stop drinking. And he did. For a while. But he started up again. He turns mean when he drinks." She knuckled away her tears. "He doesn't usually hit me in the face, but he was real mad this time. When he fell asleep, I slipped out."

Cady enfolded the other woman in her arms. "You can't go back there."

"I don't have anywhere else to go."

Cady held the woman, murmuring the soft words that came to women naturally in such circumstances.

Ford had seen women turn their lives over to their husbands. The law stripped them of their rights. They had no say over their assets, their property, even their lives.

A man could beat his wife with no fear that the law would take action. He'd seen it, had railed against it. He'd done what he could, but he couldn't change what was.

Cady took the other woman into the *Gazette,* fetched a basin of water and a cloth, and gently began tending her injured eye. She raised an eyebrow when Ford followed them inside.

Ford balled a fist. When he turned to Emilie,

though, his expression gentled. "Is there somewhere you can stay tonight?"

"She can stay with me," Cady said.

Emilie's eyes went bright and shiny at the offer. "I can't rightly do that."

He eased down beside Emilie, took her hand in his, and, careful of other bruises, ones that might be hidden, wrapped an arm around her shoulders. "Cady's right. You shouldn't be alone."

She lifted tired eyes to his. "Cal's a hard man. He don't like having someone going against him."

Ford's eyes hardened. "I'll see to him." His gaze met Cady's.

The look that passed between them was one of understanding. They both knew that Browne would continue mistreating his wife if something wasn't done to stop him. Whatever it took, they would protect Emilie. With that, a bond had been formed.

They flanked Emilie and headed to Cady's buggy. He lifted Emilie into the front seat. "I'll see you ladies home."

Cady nodded. "Thank you."

He placed his hands on her shoulders, then lowered his voice. "You may have bitten off more than you can chew."

She set her jaw. "Emilie needs a place to stay. And a friend. What are you going to do?"

"I'm going to find Cal Browne, lock him up overnight."

"Is that all? Look at her."

His lips tightened. "That's all I can do. You know what the law is."

Her nod was part acceptance, part anger. He knew what she was feeling; he was feeling the same.

He tied his horse to the back of her buggy and climbed into the driver's seat.

Though he didn't know Emilie, he cared about her, cared what happened to her. He didn't consider himself a particularly gentle man, but the woman's plight snuck behind his professional duties and into his heart.

It also threw him off his stride. He didn't like being thrown off his stride.

He snuck a glance at Cady and hoped she wouldn't stay angry with him because he couldn't promise to do more to Cal. He couldn't help the law's being what it was or people being what they were. Her compassion for Emilie softened his heart, though, and gave him a new insight into the woman.

They made the trip to the homestead in silence. Ford waited while Cady settled Emilie in her bedroom.

Cady returned to the front room. "She's sleeping. Or pretending to."

"I'll do my best to put the fear of all that's holy into Cal."

She nodded. "Any man who would abuse a helpless woman is a low-down—" She caught herself before she vented all her feelings. "Why does it have to be this way?"

He crossed the room and took her into his arms. "We're not going to solve anything tonight." He rested his chin on the top of her head.

She felt warm and womanly against him. It was that *more* that had him pulling away.

"Thanks for seeing us home," she said.

"All part of the job."

It wasn't, and they both knew it.

Ford wasn't surprised to find Cal Browne in the saloon.

A burly man, Browne was easily twice the size of his wife. He looked at Ford through bleary eyes. "You come to join us, Sheriff? We was just celebrating."

"Why?"

Browne stared at him blankly. "Why what?"

"Why were you celebrating?"

"I was telling my friends here"—he spread his arms to encompass the three men standing at the bar—"how I showed my woman who was the boss in my house." Preening, he flipped his suspenders over a filthy shirt.

The disgust that filled Ford turned to loathing. "You're an even sorrier excuse for humanity than I thought if you think that hitting a woman makes you a man." He let his gaze spread to include the other men. "And that goes for the rest of you too."

The embarrassed looks and shuffles that followed had Ford smiling without humor. "I'm glad you agree."

"You got no call talking that way to me in front of my friends." Browne's eyes glittered with meanness, and his lips peeled back in a snarl. At the same time anger washed color, red and ugly, into his face.

Ford wasn't surprised when Browne took a swing at him. Ford sidestepped and stuck out a foot. Browne tripped, landing heavily.

Ford knelt over him. Browne stank of whiskey and sweat.

"Pick him up," Ford ordered the men looking on with avid interest.

The three men picked up the dazed Browne and carted him off to jail.

Ford hadn't been able to keep Cal Browne in jail. He'd locked the man up overnight. He couldn't change the law, but he did his best to put a healthy dose of fear into Browne should he ever lay a hand on Emilie again.

"Touch her again, and I'll find a way to keep you in jail 'til we're both older than Methuselah." And then he whispered what else he'd do.

Browne's face paled beneath its layer of dirt and whiskers before he shot a surly look at Ford, one that promised retribution.

Ford had no doubt that Cady would take on Browne herself if the man tried to come near Emilie.

She reminded him of a mama raccoon—small, sturdy, and ready to fight to the death to protect her young. The more he learned about Cady, the more he found to admire. Her strength, her selflessness, her compassion were all traits he didn't often see in his line of work.

The thought of Cady's facing down a bully like Browne caused Ford's mouth to fold into a hard line. His expression softened as he thought of how she had taken Emilie into her home without a thought.

He knew that Cady didn't have much money, yet she hadn't hesitated when it came to opening her home. Or her heart. He had never been comfortable with softness, with the tenderness that some women gave so effortlessly.

His own mother had died so early. She'd been scarcely thirty when influenza had swept through the ranching community where his father had tried to eke out a living. Ford tried to bring up memories of her . . . and failed. All he had were her books.

He wished now that he could pull up a picture of her in his mind, something to remind him where he came from.

He scarcely noticed the heat of the late afternoon, his thoughts wrapped up in the past.

A bullet whizzed by, close, too close, to his head. He hit the ground, rolled, and came up with his gun drawn. "What the—" Eyes narrowed, he looked about and spotted a blond-headed boy toting a handgun.

Sonny Henriksen paled beneath the fierce glare Ford sent in his direction. "I didn't mean it. Honest, Sheriff. I was just practicin' if those rustlers come after my pa's cattle." A squeak of fear spiked the almost manly voice.

Hand trembling in reaction to what could have happened, Ford returned his gun to his holster. "You about took my head off, boy."

The gun wavered in the young hand, its weight clearly too much for the boy teetering on the edge of manhood.

Ford recalled his own first attempts with a handgun. He'd aimed it at a target and nearly shot off his foot. His pa had treated him to a trip to the woodshed, then had shown him the proper way to handle a gun.

Lars Henriksen, a Nebraska soddie, probably didn't know how to aim anything besides his old scattergun.

"Whatcha gonna do to me?" Sonny asked, his gaze skating around the hard-baked ground.

Ford checked a smile. "I'm thinking thirty days hard labor."

"Thirty whole days?"

"That's right. Sweeping out the sheriff's office." Ford fixed the boy with a stern look. "Strapping on a gun doesn't make you a man."

Sonny's face fell. "Sorry, Sheriff. I didn't mean to shoot at you."

"I know."

"You gonna tell my pa?"

"No. You are."

If possible, Sonny's face grew even more morose. "Yeah. I figured you'd say something like that. Like as not, he's gonna tan my hide."

"If he doesn't, I will."

Ford ruffled the boy's hair, pressing his lips together to hide another wayward smile. Sonny was a good kid. Ford knew the boy's father, knew he'd make sure Sonny didn't pull any more stunts like shooting a gun that few grown men could handle.

Sheriffing in a small town meant more than tracking down outlaws. It meant knowing your people and caring about them. It was that that made him realize how much he wanted to be a part of something bigger than himself.

Acceptance by the townsfolk didn't come easily. Most saw him as an upstart, trying to fill the shoes of a man who had served the town for twenty-five years. Those more charitable regarded him as a newcomer. Either way, he was an outsider, looking to belong and knowing he never would.

But he could make a difference here, now, in how he handled Sonny.

Ford thought of Sonny's parents—honest, hardworking people doing their best to eke a living out of the red clay of Colorado. Despite the hardships they faced, they were a unit.

He'd heard they'd lost a daughter the year before

to influenza. He didn't know how any parent survived such a blow. Still, the small family kept going, kept working to make a life for themselves.

The solitary existence he'd created seemed cold compared to that of those with families. Sometimes the loneliness howled through him. He reminded himself that that was the way he liked it and so was surprised to find a tug of envy pulling at him.

Wearily, he pushed it away.

Nothing lasts. The words that had guided his steps for over two decades echoed through his mind.

His ma had been dead for just over a year when a tornado cut through his family's spread, destroying everything in its wake. Thom McKinnon had fallen to his knees and wept like a baby. The house, barn, and crops had been lost. His pa had never recovered from the loss of everything. He'd died less than two years later.

Ford had learned the lesson well. *Don't get too attached to anything. Anyone. Nothing lasts.*

The encounter with Sonny brought back slices of his life he hadn't thought of in years, slices he'd actually forgotten, like his pa teaching him how to handle a gun, his ma trying to drum some manners into him.

As they had so frequently these days, his thoughts turned to Cady. He rarely entered other people's lives, but she possessed a strength and intelligence that appealed to him, and he discovered he wanted to share the incident with Sonny with her. She'd understand his feelings about keeping the boy from making the mistake of his life.

He found her at the *Gazette* and took a few moments to simply watch her. Her hair was bound back in what he supposed women called a bun. Stray curls had escaped, blurring the edges of the otherwise severe style. She tucked an errant strand behind an ear before she wiped down the press roller.

She turned, eyes widening as she registered his presence. Her gaze moved over his face, and he wondered what she saw. Instinctively, he rubbed a hand over his jaw, feeling the ridge of the scar. To Cady, he probably looked more like an outlaw than a lawman.

Her lips kicked up, drawing his attention to the dimple that flashed at one corner of her mouth. "Sheriff. Did you want something?"

He hooked his thumbs in his pockets and rocked back on his heels. "Have dinner with me," he said, surprising himself. "If we argue, I promise to let you win."

"How can I refuse?"

Chapter Four

Ford talked.

Cady listened, nodding as he told her about Sonny. "You did the right thing. There's no meanness to the boy. Only mischief and high spirits."

"That's what I thought."

Beneath duty in keeping the peace lay a very real liking for the townspeople. He respected the hard work that defined their lives, the quiet dignity that cloaked their every action, every word.

"Sam used to say that it took more than a ma and a pa to raise a child," Cady said, "that watching out for one another was what made a town."

"He was a good man." Respect and genuine liking warmed his voice.

The conversation veered to books and authors,

46

from the newcomer Twain to the classics of Shakespeare and Homer.

"You have the finest collection I've ever seen outside of a library," Cady said.

"You're welcome to borrow any of my books whenever you want."

He smiled as the idea of touching, reading, exploring his books had her catching her breath. If he'd offered her the contents of the town's only bank, he figured she couldn't have been more thrilled.

"How did you come by so many?"

"My mother loved books. They belonged to her." A wistful note edged his words.

"She died?"

"Twenty-five years ago."

"I'm sorry."

He knew she understood what it was to lose a parent. To grieve. "It was a long time ago."

"But you still miss her."

He didn't answer directly. "She was from Philadelphia. A very proper lady." His lips lifted as he recalled her telling him the story of how she and his pa had met. "She came west with my father—left everything and everyone she knew to follow him."

"She sounds like a remarkable woman."

"She was."

"My mother took off after I was born. Sam and I weren't enough to keep her."

Ford guessed that she rarely talked about her mother. If ever.

"Philadelphia is a wonderful city," she said. "When I was back East, I visited there."

Ford was perplexed with the abrupt change of subject but went along with it. "Someday I'm going there. To see the places Ma talked about."

When they finished dinner, he suggested a walk. The evening air had yet to take on the chill of autumn, and he enjoyed the slight breeze that plucked at her hair.

They walked side by side, not touching but close in an indefinable way. The sensation was a new one and not unpleasant. Not unpleasant at all. He gazed up at the streaks of red and purple in the slowly darkening sky.

Ford escorted her to the sheriff's office, where she chose a volume of poetry by Byron.

"Thank you," she said, and she ran her fingers lightly over the engraved leather cover.

"It's a pleasure to share them with someone who will appreciate them." He gave her a quizzical look. "Why a newspaper?"

"I've always been fascinated with how words shape what we think, who we are."

He noted the color that suffused her cheeks, heard the passion in her voice.

"Most people think I'm just playing at this—at putting out a newspaper. Even now, I can hardly give away ad space.

"Sam tried. He really did. But even he couldn't understand that I have to write. My friends thought it was a lark, something I'd grow tired of in a few months."

"Then they don't know you very well," he said, moved by the simple pleasure on her face. He had no business making such a personal comment and decided to steer the conversation in another direction. "How's Emilie getting along?"

"Good. She's working for me. I'm teaching her how to set type."

"Do you ever get frightened, living so far out of town?"

She shook her head. "There's no one who would hurt me."

"What about Cal Browne?"

Mention of Emilie's husband had her smile dimming. Browne had made no secret of his dislike for Cady or his determination to get his wife back. So far, it was only talk.

Cal was a bully, and, in Ford's experience, bullies were cowards, but he made a mental note to keep track of the man all the same.

"He doesn't scare me."

"Maybe he should."

The terseness of his reply erased the rest of her smile. "I can take care of myself."

"If he bothers you, let me know. Please."

Perhaps it was the entreaty of the last word that had her nodding.

"You could get a lot of people's backs up, taking Emilie in the way you did."

"I didn't take in Emilie to win any popularity contests."

"No. I don't suppose you did."

Ford knew that Cady's offer to let Emilie stay with her had made the gossip rounds. Some of the townspeople now regarded Cady with thinly veiled animosity.

More than a few thought as Browne did. A man's wife was his property, his to do with as he saw fit. Many a man afforded his animals better treatment than he did his woman. Only a few had offered support, and that was done in hushed tones.

He'd heard that the livery station owner had withdrawn his ad from the *Gazette*. He doubted that Cady could afford the loss of revenue, but he knew she wouldn't turn Emilie out.

His lips thinned as he thought of Emilie's swollen lip and black eye.

"Thank you for dinner," Cady said.

"It was my pleasure."

Ford saw her back to her ranch after that. He jumped down from the buggy, then reached up to help her. He brushed a finger over her cheek. "Good night, Cady. Thank you for spending the evening with me."

Emilie was waiting up, her eyes bright with excitement when Cady let herself inside. "The sheriff brought you home."

Cady removed her shawl and hung it on a peg. "We had dinner at the cafe."

And they had talked.

Cady hadn't enjoyed a conversation so much in longer than she could remember. Ford was not only intelligent, he also had a way with words that fascinated her, making her want to capture the flavor of his speech on paper.

Anxious to turn her thoughts in a different direction, she let her gaze skim the room, noting the touches Emilie had brought to the cabin. Wildflowers in a fruit jar graced the rough table. The curtains at the kitchen window had received a recent laundering and ironing.

Despite Cady's protests, Emilie insisted upon doing the washing and the ironing. There was the clean, dry smell of fresh linen as she carefully folded one of Cady's shirtwaists.

"You can stay as long as you want," Cady said whenever Emilie made noises about moving out.

"I can't rightly do that. You've done too much already."

"I haven't done anything. You need a place to stay. I have room. It's as simple as that."

Emilie planted her hands on her hips. "I need to earn my keep."

"You already have."

In the past week, Emilie had blossomed. Away from her husband and with a job she enjoyed, she had taken a new interest in everything, including, it seemed, Cady's personal life. "What's happening with you and the sheriff?"

"We're friends."

"I've seen how he looks at you. Did he kiss you good night?"

Cady felt her cheeks heat with color. "No."

Emilie gave Cady an impatient look. "There's something between you and him."

The words hit Cady like a dousing of cold water, and she took refuge in briskness. "Ford and I enjoy each other's company. That's all." She knew she sounded crisp, even a little defensive. Not for the world would she admit that the new sheriff was occupying her thoughts to an annoying degree.

"He's different than anyone I've ever known," she admitted. There was more, so much more, but she couldn't find the words. Nor did she want to. The feelings Ford roused within her were special, too special to share, even with her friend.

A private man, Ford didn't give away much. Only when he talked about books had he opened up. She realized she wanted to know more about him, to learn more about the man who was as comfortable discussing poetry as he was handling a gun.

She had her opportunity to do just that at a town meeting the following night. The schoolhouse, which also served as the church, functioned as the town hall as well. She found a place near the front of the room where she could observe the proceedings.

She tried not to notice how good it felt to watch Ford walk into the room. She noticed the way his eyes constantly scanned right and left, the way he rolled off the balls of his feet. His arms hung loosely at his sides, pushing him along but never far from his body.

Though he looked completely at ease—casual, even—she knew that his every action had a purpose. She doubted anyone else noticed the lines of tension around his eyes.

Except Cady knew he was feeling anything but casual. There was an undercurrent of strength that ran through the man, and it never let up. He gave the impression of being relaxed, but his eyes were alert, always watching, picking up every detail and dissecting.

In that moment, she understood how he'd earned his reputation. It wasn't his prowess with a gun, though that was formidable. It wasn't the badge, though he wore it with a quiet authority that inspired confidence and trust.

It was the man himself.

Where had that come from? she wondered. She scarcely knew him, but she sensed he was a good man, one who had made his own way and went his own way, no matter what others thought.

She shifted, annoyed and frustrated without being

able to identify why. She only knew he had a way of drawing out those reactions in her. He had a way about him that made a woman notice him.

He took a seat with the mayor at the front of the room.

Mayor Gardner stood. "I want to thank you good people for coming here tonight," he said to the assembled townsfolk. He cleared his throat, a sure sign he was about to launch into one of his long-winded speeches.

"Sit down, and let the sheriff talk," one of the local ranchers said.

At the cheers from the crowd, the mayor offered a grudging smile and took his seat.

"Sheriff, tell us what you're doing to rid our town of these varmints."

"Yeah," another man seconded. "We need protection. We ain't seen none of that fancy reputation we hired you for."

A muscle in Ford's jaw ticked.

Most people wouldn't have noticed anything unusual in his reaction. In fact, he covered his emotions so well that most would probably swear he hadn't reacted at all.

Cady supposed that was one of the things that made him such a good sheriff. She watched his physical responses with the experienced eye of a professional observer. Every muscle tensed. Each breath came faster and shallower than the last.

He didn't rush but got to his feet slowly. Whatever had annoyed him had been quickly and ruthlessly banked. He took his time, letting his gaze roam over the audience. "You didn't hire a reputation. You hired a man. Me. If any of you have a problem with that, you'd better let me know now, and I'll resign."

The mayor, along with some of the others in the audience, made protesting sounds.

Ford waited until the clatter of voices subsided. "The rustling started before I got here. It didn't spring up overnight. And it won't be solved overnight."

"You talk real pretty," the second man said. "But you still ain't given us anything that's gonna keep our stock safe."

"You want me to keep your spreads safe. Let me tell you what I need. I need your eyes and ears. Let me know if you see anything suspicious. Talk with your neighbors. Keep an eye out for them. This is a town problem, and it will be solved by the town. Not by one man alone."

Murmurs of approval rippled through the crowd. Cady made notes, at the same time silently applauding Ford's challenge.

He had admitted his lack of progress in solving the rustling. He hadn't tried to cover it up or make excuses. Then he'd tossed it back to the ranchers, inviting them to work with him to put an end to the problem.

Her admiration grew as she watched him. The new sheriff had a lot going for him.

He cared about others. She'd heard of how he went out of his way to help anyone in need. Word of it had spread. Colorado Springs didn't have any secrets.

Lars Henriksen sang his praises any chance he could for the way Ford had handled Sonny. "A good man is that one," Lars had said in his heavily accented English. "He does our town proud."

Cady could only agree. Ford did their town proud.

Because he didn't say a lot, you listened when he did. And when it came time to act, he did what was needed without drawing attention to it.

It was an appealing brand of self-confidence that contained not a whit of arrogance.

His eyes were steady and clear, radiating integrity and strength. He was, she realized in a flash, a man you could count on.

He moved with a quiet grace that was at odds with his size. He didn't hurry, but you got the impression that, if the need arose, he could move fast and move hard.

She stored away the impressions to take out later and sort through.

The aloofness that normally characterized her reaction to a man was conspicuously absent. It didn't improve her mood to realize she'd spent the last few minutes doing nothing but staring at the new sheriff.

She raised her gaze and caught his smile, one that said he was aware of what she was doing.

Ford McKinnon was an unusual man. Everything

she had learned about him so far confirmed that and made her want to learn more.

After the meeting was over, he made his way toward her. "Cady. May I see you home?"

Something hovered near her heart. "I'd like that."

Ford tied his mount behind the buggy, then helped her into it. He rubbed a hand over the stubble that was beginning to darken his jaw.

The drive through town took both less and more time than she wanted. She noticed the cluster of people who had gathered at the open-air cafe, the center of town life, and knew they would be chewing over the town meeting and the new sheriff.

Doris waved a greeting, then directed a glance at Cady's companion. Cady could see the open curiosity in the other woman's eyes and turned her head so that she could meet Ford's gaze.

His face twisted briefly in a wry smile. "Have you noticed how many eyes are on us?"

"Do you mind?"

He shook his head. "Not really. How about you?"

Her huff was half laughter. "I grew up here. I gave up the idea of privacy when I was twelve and Sam swatted my bottom in front of the whole town for sassing him."

One corner of his mouth dipped, emphasizing the cleft in his chin. She longed to trace that slight indentation. With a barely suppressed gasp, she realized she had raised her fingers to do just that.

She dropped her hand.

The fading light of the day burnished his dark hair, the strong bones of his face, the breadth of his shoulders.

Ford turned to her. "You've been itching to say something ever since we left the meeting."

"I like how you handle yourself. You say what you mean without a lot of fancy words attached. That goes a long way with folks around here."

He looked surprised. "Thanks."

Chapter Five

The following morning, Cady yanked her brush through her hair with impatient strokes. Giving up, she bundled it into a knot at her neck, not caring that most of it had escaped the pins she ruthlessly jammed into it.

She drove the buggy to town with none of her customary cheer, barely mumbling a half dozen sentences to Emilie. At the paper, her mind wandered, her concentration nil; her eyes kept straying to the clock. And all she could think of was Ford and the feel of his arms last night.

She looked up to find Emilie regarding her speculatively. Her friend was grinning as if she had a secret she didn't intend to share.

Cady turned her attention to setting up the press.

The machine sputtered and coughed, and she feared it needed more repairs—money she couldn't spare.

She coaxed the press into working and experienced her customary thrill at seeing the first paper emerge.

Next came her favorite part.

Cady like delivering the paper. It was then she could talk with the townspeople and keep current about what was happening. Too, she enjoyed the personal contact. Much of the success in putting out a town paper depended upon knowing the people.

Her deliveries completed, she headed back to the *Gazette*. Her eyes narrowed as she saw Calvin Browne, a sneer pulling his lips down, approach.

She held her ground against the man's mean glower, refusing to take a step back, though her instincts urged her to do just that. Browne was the worst kind of man, one who would sense weakness and exploit it.

"I heard you have my wife staying with you." Browne's face crimsoned. "She belongs at home. With her man."

He shifted his weight, leaning toward her. Again she fought the impulse to put more space between them. She wouldn't give in to his blatant attempt to intimidate her.

"She belongs in a place where she'll be treated with respect." Cady let her gaze rake the man. "Any man who hits a woman doesn't deserve the name."

Browne took her arm in a bruising grip. "What would your pa say about your sticking your nose into something that weren't none of your business?"

"He'd say to make sure I knew what I was doing and then get on with it." Cady attempted to shake off his hand but couldn't budge it. "Let go of me."

"Not until you start minding your own business," he said, his voice more menacing than ever. His nostrils flared. "You send Emilie packing, or   "

Browne never got the satisfaction of finishing his threat.

Ford shouldered himself between Cady and the other man, legs spread, shoulders squared, braced to defend or attack, whichever became necessary. "The lady told you to let go of her."

So close was Browne that she could smell the whiskey on his breath.

Browne abruptly freed her arm. "The lady and I were just having ourselves a talk. No harm done." He took himself off, but not without a last malevolent look in her direction.

Cady drew a steadying breath.

Ford took a look at her and then spun her around, shielding her from the view of curious onlookers. He didn't say anything but gave her time to pull herself together.

Her breathing evened out, and she noticed things about him. His linsey-woolsey shirt was darkened with perspiration, the sleeves rolled up to reveal arms that were ropey with muscle and sinew. Sunlight caught the sheen of sweat that glossed his skin.

She stared, trying not to notice how solid and strong he looked, trying not to think about the good, male scent of him, trying not to focus on the fullness of his lips.

She thought of what might have happened if Ford hadn't come along and shook her head to dispel the image. "Browne's a bigger idiot than I thought."

Ford nodded. "Good. You've got your sass back."

"Thank you. If you hadn't come along . . ."

"Blame it on my mother."

"Your mother?"

"She taught me that a gentleman always comes to the aid of a lady."

"And are you? A gentleman?"

"I try." He hooked an arm around her waist and drew her close. The steady beat of his heart mingled with her erratic one. "I'll see you back to your office."

"Thanks."

Outside the *Gazette,* he stopped. "Friends?"

"Friends."

"Prove it."

"How?"

"Let me take you to the town dance Saturday night."

It was a challenge, one he didn't expect her to accept. Maybe it was that, he thought, that prompted her to say yes, and maybe it was more basic than that—the attraction that had existed between them from the start.

"I . . . I don't know."

"Scared?"

That had her squaring her shoulders. "I'll meet you there."

He shook his head. "We'll do it right." He brushed something that might have been a kiss across her cheek. "I'll pick you up Saturday night."

Cady walked into the office, wondering if she were more shaken from her run-in with Cal or from Ford's almost-kiss. "Sorry I'm late," she said to Emilie.

"Is something wrong?"

Cady wasn't about to tell Emilie that Cal had accosted her. "Ford asked me to the Sweetheart Dance."

Emilie clapped her hands. "The Sweetheart Dance." Her eyes went dreamy. Even after her experience, Emilie remained a romantic at heart.

"I don't have a dress."

"I'd lend you one of mine, but it would never fit." Cady barely reached Emilie's chin. "Tomorrow we go shopping."

Cady nearly groaned. She'd rather walk barefoot across the desert than go shopping for a dress.

She noticed Emilie stifling a yawn. "Why don't you get something at the cafe? I'll finish up here and meet you there."

Alone, Cady was assailed by doubts over agreeing to accompany Ford to the town dance, and she knew it had nothing to do with her lack of a proper dress.

What had she been thinking in accepting the invitation? She had no answer to that—at least, no good answer. With an impatient shake of her head, she shrugged off her preoccupation with a certain dark-haired sheriff and methodically began going through the mail that accumulated each day.

She worked through the next half hour with no interruptions. As the evening shadows lengthened, she leaned back in her chair and closed her eyes. Though she would have died before admitting it, she was thinking of Ford.

The next day, Emilie bullied Cady into a trip to the General Mercantile. They found a pale blue dress that did flattering things to her fair hair and skin.

The evening of the dance, Emilie gathered Cady's hair into soft curls that brushed her shoulders. A touch of lemon verbena at her throat and wrists provided an added touch of femininity. Nothing could remove the ink stains from her hands, though, and she didn't try. More than anything, they defined who and what she was.

"You're beautiful," Emilie said with a last adjustment to Cady's hair.

"I'm passable," Cady corrected, but she couldn't stop the small thrill of knowing she looked her best.

Magic touched the air when Ford knocked on the door. With hands suddenly gone damp, she opened it.

His gaze moved over her. He looked blank for a moment, like a man who had forgotten what he was doing in the middle of a task. The knowledge that she had done that both surprised and thrilled her.

"Cady." His voice was soft and rough at the same time.

Her name on his lips warmed her. At the same time, a shiver whispered over her arms. How could he produce two such contradictory reactions in her?

No man she'd ever known came close to Ford in terms of masculine appeal. He had the kind of presence that came from feeling comfortable in his own skin.

More handsome than ever in a white shirt and dark trousers, he gave a low whistle. His slow smile caused her stomach to grow jittery. The look in his eyes made every cent she'd spent on the dress worth it. It was the first time he had directed such undisguised admiration in her direction.

The idea that this man could somehow be fighting the same attraction for her that she felt for him was a heady one. Drawn by a force against which she had no control, she felt herself leaning toward him.

She prepared to enjoy herself. No talk of the rustling or Calvin Browne would mar the evening. A ribbon of anticipation curled through her at the thought of dancing with Ford.

The evening breeze raised goose bumps on her arms, despite her shawl, and she shivered. Ford settled his arm around her, handling the buggy reins easily with one hand.

After helping her from the buggy, Ford tucked her hand into the crook of his arm. She heard the murmurs as they made their entrance and smiled to herself. They'd set the tongues to wagging tonight for sure.

Women, both married and unmarried, eyed Ford with poorly concealed interest and all but melted at his smile. Instinctively, Cady tightened her hold on his arm, surprised at the spurt of jealousy that slid through her.

A fiddler and square-dance caller provided the music. Ford led her onto the makeshift dance floor. They do-si-doed and danced the reel with the rest of the crowd.

Breathless, she lifted her gaze to his and was stopped by the warmth in his eyes.

"Let's get some punch," he said, using his shoulders to break a path through the crowd.

Cady felt as if everyone in the room watched as they made their way to the refreshment table. Open stares, not-so-subtle glances, and an audible hush followed their slow progress through the throng of dancers.

She caught the envious glances the other women shot her way. She didn't blame them. Ford made an impressive figure in his dark trousers and snowy shirt. She noticed the way his muscles moved beneath his clothing.

It wasn't just his size, though that was impressive. It wasn't just his beautifully molded lips, though they were certainly appealing. It wasn't even the eyes, though their dark watchfulness made her aware of him . . . and of herself as a woman.

Sarah Gardner, the mayor's daughter, watched them with narrowed eyes. "Don't you look nice tonight, Cady? So different than your usual getups."

Ford smiled. "Cady's lovely no matter what she's wearing."

He meant it, and wasn't that a miracle? Cady had never thought of herself as particularly pretty. She was passable looking. No more. No less. But Ford thought she was special. She'd felt it in his touch, heard it in his voice.

A faint frown crossed Sarah's pretty face. The mayor's daughter was accustomed to being the center of attention at any town function, partly because of her father's position but mostly because she was a beautiful girl.

Cady couldn't help a moment's pleasure that Ford had asked her to the dance rather than Sarah.

They turned their attention to the refreshments. The town ladies had outdone themselves. Sorghum-flavored cookies, apple pan dowdy, and a score of other treats lined the table.

The evening seemed dusted with magic. The food was plentiful, the music lively, the man at her side attentive. After sampling the food, they rejoined the other dancers.

Turning her head, Cady could see the strong line of his jaw, the sun-bronzed gold of his skin. She felt hard muscle where her hand rested lightly on his shoulder.

His hand firm at her waist, Ford guided her through the motions of the reel. The air hummed with tension, an awareness she couldn't deny.

She put her hand in his. His long, tanned fingers wrapped around her own, a protective gesture that wasn't lost on her.

Cady stumbled and would have fallen if not for Ford's support. Mortification burned through her, painting her cheeks with hot color. "I'm sorry. I'm not very good at this dancing stuff."

"You're doing just fine."

"Why did you ask me? To the dance?"

"Because I like being with you. Is that so hard to believe?"

"Yes," she said frankly. "I wear ink on my hands and clothes and work with machines all day. I'm not like Sarah or the other women."

"No," he said. "You're not."

He made it sound like the loveliest of compliments. Once more her cheeks heated, but it was with pleasure this time.

When they weren't dancing, they mingled with the other couples. Never comfortable with small talk, Cady still managed to hold her own.

When a ranch hand from the Gardner spread asked her to dance, she accepted. He whirled her away.

Flushed after several more dances, Cady started toward the refreshment table, where Ford waited.

Mayor Gardner waylaid her. "You're looking mighty fetchin' tonight."

"Thank you, Mayor." She gave a small curtsy.

"Mighty fetchin'." He caught the glare his wife sent his way and trotted off in her direction.

"It looks as if Mrs. Gardner doesn't like her husband paying court to anyone but her," Ford observed.

"You've got part of it right. Sarah is the belle of every dance in Colorado Springs. Mrs. Gardner doesn't like anyone else stealing attention from her daughter." She blushed. "I didn't mean . . ."

"You're right but for one thing. Sarah *was* the belle." Ford emphasized the past tense, then drew her into his arms for the final dance, the "Sweetheart Waltz."

He held her closely, as though he could keep out the rest of the world. For the space of the dance, he succeeded. There was only the two of them. Her head pressed to his shoulder, she was aware of only him and the attraction humming between them.

"You're beautiful," he whispered.

The two words produced a warm, fluttering sensation inside her. Emilie had uttered the same words, but Cady had shrugged them off. Now she held them to her heart.

When the music lapsed into silence, Cady hardly noticed, so caught up had she been in the sensation of being in Ford's arms.

His arm was warm around her waist. He didn't bother to remove it.

She didn't bother to mention it.

They made their good-byes to the others in attendance.

Ford held her shawl for her, his hands cupping her shoulders and lingering there before he escorted her outside.

He helped her into the buggy, then climbed in beside her. He drove a short distance from town, then pulled the buggy to a stop. His fingers traced a path down her cheek. "There's something I've been wanting to do all night."

She knew what was coming. The intent in his eyes was too obvious, the shortness of his breath too clear.

She had only enough time to breathe his name before his lips settled over hers. She swayed against him and closed her eyes, knowing the kiss would be gentle.

It was.

The touch of his lips on hers sent her thoughts scattering like dry leaves caught in a November wind. The kiss was a meeting of lips but so much more, and she was powerless to resist it.

His breath was warm and sweet against her face,

his hands strong as they held her. She registered all that and more.

For the span of a heartbeat, a single, endless moment, time ground to a standstill. A slow, sure smile appeared upon his lips, quickening her pulse. She moistened suddenly dry lips and swallowed while her heart tumbled in her chest, a slow roll that had her gripping his shoulders more tightly.

Cady shivered. Whether it was from pleasure or the chill that accompanied the breeze didn't seem to matter. What mattered was that he held her as if he never intended to let her go.

She'd been kissed before, but never like this. This kiss was the stuff dreams were made of. She returned it with shy enthusiasm.

Then, as if neither had a choice, the kiss deepened, turned endless and needful.

Her heart gave a nervous jerk. At the same time she felt curiously breathless. She inhaled deeply, needing to clear her mind. She was aware of every pore, every nerve. Each seemed to draw taut.

Cady realized she'd been holding her breath and forced herself to draw a gulp of air. Her world finally righted itself, and she flushed at the extent of her feelings for this man she had known such a short time.

When she lifted her head, she smiled at him. "That was nice." It was more than nice, but she didn't have the words. Curious, she thought. She made her living with words, but they failed her now.

A thimble-sized breeze stirred the edges of his part. She reached up to smooth his hair back into place, and as she touched him, their eyes met and held.

The silence as they rode home was a comforting one. Her head, though, was spinning. It had been years since she'd felt this kind of attraction to a man. Invitations to church suppers or Sunday picnics had been plentiful, but she hadn't been interested.

Her dream had occupied her full attention. No man could compete with the thought of operating her own newspaper.

Until now.

She hadn't realized it, but she'd been waiting. Waiting for someone special. Waiting for Ford.

They made the remainder of the trip to her cabin in silence. Ford saw her to the door, then touched his lips lightly to hers once more. "I'll see you tomorrow."

She could only nod. Once inside, she brought her shawl to her nose and inhaled deeply.

It bore his scent.

Chapter Six

In Colorado Springs, when a subject was on some-body's mind, it was most likely on everyone's mind. Being on everybody's mind, it became fair game for gossip, and gossip was what the townspeople did best, in depth and in public.

Cady was used to it. What she wasn't accustomed to was being the subject of that gossip. So, when she saw Doc Shultz nursing a cup of coffee at the open-air cafe, she made a point of asking him about the McGurdys' baby. There was nothing that claimed the doctor's attention more than talking about delivering a new life.

"Breeched," he said with a look that made it plain he knew what Cady was doing. "It's a miracle Hannah and the baby are both all right, him weighing in at over eight pounds."

Cady made the appropriate comments, satisfied that she'd derailed the doc's curiosity.

"Heard you and the sheriff were stepping out together," Doc said as she took a sip of her coffee.

Cady managed—barely—not to choke on the hot liquid. So much for thinking she'd distracted Doc. "You heard that, did you?" She put just enough vinegar into her voice to let her irritation show.

"Don't go getting all closemouthed on me," Doc chided, his unruly brows coming together. "You and McKinnon can't be sparking and not have everyone in town know about it."

Cady knew, but that didn't mean she had to like it. Still, she didn't have it in her to snub her old friend. She put down her coffee and turned a smile on him. Doc was pushing seventy, yet he kept up his large practice without breaking stride.

"I have a hankering for some of Doris' pie," she said, "but I don't feel like eating alone. Will you join me?"

Doc looked pleased. "Can't say that wouldn't sit right good."

Cady gave something between a snort and a chuckle. She'd never known Doc to turn down a piece of pie. When Doris reappeared, Cady put in an order.

There was no question about what flavor of pie

they'd order. Doris Conway, who had owned and operated the cafe ever since Cady could remember, made one kind and one kind only. Cherry. Attempts to convince her to add to the menu had met with steadfast resistance.

With small-town pride, the customers had adjusted, even bragging about Doris' cherry pie. It was but one more part of living in the Springs.

"Secrets are hard to keep here in the Springs," Doris said, unashamed of her obvious eavesdropping. "Especially when it's the new sheriff and Sam's daughter who're doing the sparkin'."

Cady gave a resigned sigh. "I know."

Doris looked amused. "Folks in town are thinking you two will make a match of it."

"Make a mighty fine-looking couple," Doc added.

Cady looked at her friends with exasperation and affection, knowing their meddling was prompted by genuine caring. She endured a few more questions before Doris moved on.

Doc rambled on with stories Cady had heard a dozen times before. Because Cady liked him and would have done anything rather than hurt his feelings, she listened with rapt attention.

Companionably, they finished their coffee and pie.

After pushing his plate away, Doc got to his feet. "You're a good gal. Time you found yourself a fellow and settled down and started making babies. No charge for the first one," he added with a wink. "If I were fifty years younger, you'd have to beat off the other fellers with a stick."

Cady gave the expected grin, but her thoughts were on Ford and the kiss they'd shared. She'd held on to the memory of that kiss long after it ended.

Back at the *Gazette,* she closed the door and leaned against it.

Emilie looked up from cleaning the press cylinder. "Did you have a good time last night?"

To Cady's relief, Emilie had been asleep when Cady returned home after the dance. It had spared her from answering questions.

She made a noncommittal *hmm*.

When Emilie tapped her foot, Cady blushed. "All right. I had a good time. Ford—Sheriff McKinnon—" She broke off and frowned at Emilie, who grinned at her with obvious delight. "What's so funny?"

Emilie gave a look of abject innocence. "Nothing. I was going to ask if he kissed you good night, but I think I have my answer."

Cady sighed. Over the last weeks the two women had become friends. That was the problem with friends—nothing was out-of-bounds.

"It was a town dance. That's all," she said, then wondered just who needed the reminder more, Emilie or herself?

She remembered how it felt to have Ford's arms around her, his lips a scant inch from her own.

Emilie cleared her throat and, for the first time since she'd started to work for Cady, looked uncomfortable. "It's time I found my own place."

Cady stared at her friend in surprise. She'd grown accustomed to sharing the cabin with someone else and had enjoyed the company, but she understood that Emilie needed a place of her own. "Have you thought about where you'll go?"

Emilie shook her head. "I can't afford much."

"I could come up with a few extra dollars." Cady gave a silent apology to her already sagging bank balance.

Emilie gave another emphatic shake of her head. "It's time I started standing on my own feet."

"There are a couple of rooms here." Cady glanced at the second floor of the *Gazette* office. They had remained empty, though she had dreams of expanding the paper someday.

"I'd have to pay you."

Cady wanted to refuse but knew Emilie needed to pay her own way. "Of course."

Emilie's face relaxed into a smile that came more easily these days. "Thank you." She gave Cady a quick, hard hug. "For everything."

"I'll miss you."

"We'll still see each other every day."

With Ford's promise to come by when she got off work, the afternoon sped by. Cady staunchly denied her disappointment when he failed to show up.

The sheriff was a busy man, with responsibilities to the town and its people, she reminded herself. Of course he didn't have time to stop by the *Gazette* just to talk with her.

With that, she could view the situation between herself and Ford more rationally. They were attracted to each other. That didn't mean they had any claim on each other.

Together, she and Emilie completed the editing, then the painstaking task of typesetting.

With renewed determination, she put Ford out of her mind and wrote her latest editorial, this one focusing on national politics. Though many considered Colorado far removed from Washington, Cady included events from the nation's capital in the paper whenever possible.

Cady turned to Emilie. "You might as well get something to eat. I'm going to be here awhile longer."

"Are you sure?"

"Go, before I change my mind."

Over the next hour, Cady wrote and rewrote. She cranked the press. The familiar sound reassured her.

She accidentally scraped her fingers on the rough edge of the underbelly of the press. She flexed her hands. The skin smarted and burned but not enough to interfere with her work.

She heard the door open. Believing it to be Emilie, she didn't bother looking up. "Didn't I tell you to get something to eat?"

"No."

She spun around, flustered to find Ford watching her. He *would* come now, when her hair hung in damp tendrils on her neck, her cheeks were shiny with sweat, her fingers covered with ink. She lifted a hand to swipe at a loose strand of hair that clung to her jaw.

"What've you done to yourself?"

She gave a wry smile. "I had an argument with the printing press. It won."

He fetched a bowl, filled it with water from the pump out back, and gently bathed her fingers.

The scrapes didn't warrant such attention—she'd had worse—but the gentleness of his ministrations touched her in an unexpected way. Gentleness and strength in a man were a potent combination, and she wasn't immune to the force of it.

"Does it hurt?"

She shook her head, unable to trust her voice. She could feel nothing but the touch of his hand on hers, the warmth, the caring. "I'm not used to being fussed over."

"I'm tending to your hand. That's all." His tenderness said otherwise.

"I'm not some fragile city woman. I've skinned myself up before, and I'll probably do it again."

He finished bathing her hand, then gently dried it with a clean rag. "You work too hard."

"When I get the paper to put itself out, I'll let up. Until then, I don't have much choice."

She'd spoken only the truth. Sam hadn't pampered her. He'd seen that she had the tools and the knowledge to take care of herself, then had let her do just that. Ford's concern over a simple scrape puzzled her.

"Play hooky with me for the rest of the afternoon."

She hesitated.

"Please."

She couldn't think of anything she'd rather do than spend the afternoon with Ford. "Yes." She walked with him to the stable where he kept his horses during the day.

Ford led a seventeen-hand gelding out of a stall.

Cady found herself entranced by the beautifully built animal who had a bearing that spoke of his breeding. The muscles of his hindquarters moved fluidly beneath a coat that shone from hours of grooming. As though aware of his status as center of attention, he tossed his head and pranced.

"Meet Hawk. Hawk, make nice to the lady." A nod of the big head had her smiling. He nuzzled her neck, causing her to laugh.

Ford gestured to the neighboring stall, which housed a dainty mare. "Meet Frosty. I bought her as company for Hawk."

Cady patted the mare on the neck and was rewarded with an enthusiastic whinny. "She's a beauty."

He saddled Frosty for her and Hawk for himself. They set an easy pace, enjoying the ride and each other's company.

Cady's gaze slid his way more than once as she admired the way his body rose and fell in rhythm with the horse's gait. Her thoughts drifted to the previous evening.

He looked up once and caught her watching him. For a moment, she imagined she knew what he was thinking. He didn't smile, didn't say anything, but something in the depth of his gaze told her that he, too, was remembering what it felt like to hold her.

What unnerved her most were those moments when she caught him studying her with an oddly wistful expression in his eyes, an expression that always disappeared the moment he realized she had noticed.

His hand in a glove that smelled sharp with sweat and use, he reached across Hawk's withers to brush Cady's fingers. Even through the leather of her own worn gloves, she imagined she could feel his touch.

The day was a shiny one. Cady smiled as she recalled the phrase from her childhood. Sam had called the frequent hot, cloudless days of Colorado summers "shiny days." The sun shimmered off the land, and she had to squint against its unrelenting glare.

It was nice, she thought, to share such a day with Ford. Today was a day for dreams to come true. A day to forget the past, ignore the future, and simply live every moment as it came.

No, the high plains weren't for everyone. Their

beauty was a demanding one. No rolling hills or leaf-laden trees like those she had seen in the East softened the harsh edges of the land. It bespoke strength, exacting a matching one from those who chose to make their homes there.

Cady swept her hat back, letting the wind have its way with her hair.

They rode with an unexpected camaraderie. She matched her rhythm to that of her mount and enjoyed the easy pace Ford set, the song the wind made, the sunlight dappling the ground.

She felt herself relaxing, enjoying the company, the time away from the *Gazette*. Though she loved her work, she couldn't deny the pressures of putting out a newspaper.

The mare moved with easy grace, her nostrils twitching in the dry wind that swept over the prairie, ears pricked forward. She was a prize, dainty head held high, sleek muscles quivering at Cady's slightest touch.

Ford helped her dismount, letting his hands linger for seconds longer than necessary on her waist. He opened a bag filled with oats for the horses.

She liked that he had thought of the horses. Sam had claimed that you could tell a lot about a man by the care he took of his animals.

Ford was achingly aware of her and caught himself wanting to reach out to touch her hair, her shoulder, her hand.

Her hair lifted on a whiff of breeze and floated back to gently tease his lips. He gave in to the impulse to smooth it back into place. As he did so, his thumb grazed her cheek. The feel of her skin nearly undid him.

Ford took the saddlebag from Hawk and slung it over his shoulder. His other hand found Cady's.

The strength and ease with which she strode over the rough ground told him she wasn't a stranger to the mountains. As she had pointed out, she wasn't fragile. Cady, for all her small size, was no pampered city miss. But then, he had never had any interest in delicate women who couldn't handle themselves.

Not since Margaret, anyway.

He hadn't thought of his old sweetheart in a long time. Years ago he'd asked Margaret, a pretty school-teacher from back East, to marry him. She'd accepted.

Then he'd been wounded in the shoulder. To her credit, Margaret had stayed at his side while he recovered. She'd then told him she couldn't marry him. He didn't blame her. Gently reared, she had no experience with the harsh realities he faced every day.

He reminded himself that he wasn't looking for anything more than friendship with Cady. He had seen too many peace officers leave a wife and family behind to risk inflicting that kind of pain on anyone.

He'd stayed heart-whole ever since.

The glen was a sweet refuge of greenery and shade.

Ford spread a blanket over a carpet of springy grass, then opened the brown-paper-wrapped food. "Doris made it up for me."

They shared fried chicken, cornbread squares, and thick wedges of pie.

"Cherry," they said in unison.

His laughter came fast and rich. He stood and walked to the edge of the glen.

She joined him. She didn't say anything, seeming to understand his need for quiet. She had an infinite capacity for stillness. A man who valued the peace of quiet, he appreciated that.

Never had he known a woman so totally attuned to what he was feeling. He realized he was beginning to take such silences for granted. He didn't worry about offending her when he pulled into himself and let his thoughts drift.

It was he who finally broke the silence. "The Cheyenne say this is where heaven and earth come to talk each day."

"What do they talk about?"

"Anything. Everything." He touched her cheek. "Men and women and how they feel about each other."

Ford watched the play of emotions across her features. He wondered if she knew just how much of herself she revealed in her eyes. He doubted it. With her red-gold hair, she reminded him of the desert at sunset.

He drew her to him. She fit against him as though she had been made for that sole purpose, yet she was tiny enough that he could tuck her into his pocket.

She not only felt good against him, but right. With some surprise, he realized this was the first time he'd ever known simple contentment in a woman's company.

With Cady, he felt no pressure, only a sense of rightness that they should be together.

It had been impossible not to be aware of how she'd looked in the fragile blue dress on the night of the dance. Although she probably wasn't conscious of the impression she made, he was. He'd seen prettier women, but not one had made the impression Cady had. There, with sunlight in her hair turning it to the color of dark honey, he felt his heart take a tumble.

Until Cady Armstrong had entered his life, he'd been satisfied with the way things were. It had been a long time since he'd thought about sharing his life with anyone, let alone a strong-willed, opinionated woman like Cady.

Now, in the beauty of the Colorado setting, he let his imagination take flight. The setting couldn't be more perfect for spinning dreams. The thin, high clouds were turning rose against a turquoise sky. The distant mountains gave fresh meaning to the word *majestic*. Sage and mustard weed provided splashes of color to brighten the rugged landscape. The sight, he thought, was a peaceful thing for a man to behold.

It was a world of contrasts, scrub brush and towering pines, temperatures that plummeted to below freezing and heat intense enough to fry eggs on a rock.

She followed his gaze. "It soothes the soul, doesn't it?"

Beauty did soothe the soul, he thought. With Cady at his side and the spectacular vista stretched forth before him, he was surrounded by it.

"Home," she said quietly.

He looked at her, then quickly looked away. But the word lingered with him. *Home*.

He was surprised how natural it felt sharing with her the place he'd discovered shortly after coming to Colorado Springs, sharing an intimacy that came upon them unaware. To his surprise, he found himself telling Cady how he'd never had a sense of belonging after his pa died.

"I keep looking. Wanting. Waiting."

She closed her hands over his. "Maybe you've found it." As though startled by the sound of her own voice, she stood stock-still.

He watched as Cady cleared away the bits and pieces of their picnic remains, stowing them in the saddlebags. He liked that she didn't leave trash to clutter the landscape. She knew what mattered. And what didn't.

She didn't fuss that her dress bore a smudge of dirt or that her hair had come undone from a braid. But she cared—cared deeply—about people.

Ford plucked a blade of long grass and chewed on it thoughtfully.

She turned to him, her eyes alight with happiness. "Why did you bring me here?"

He knew his answer would change the direction of their relationship, but he didn't hesitate. "Because I wanted you here. I like it here, and I wanted you to like it too."

He took her hand in his. His words wrapped around her heart just as his hand wrapped around hers. And her heart melted.

"Thank you," she said. "For sharing it with me."

"I like you, Cady. It's time you accepted that."

She didn't know what she felt. About this man. About herself. How could she? Her experience was limited at best.

Their gazes locked and held. He was the one to break it, to give that crooked smile that never failed to raise a response within her.

Things were moving too fast. Emilie's words came back to tease her mind, and she shrank from finding out if they were true.

The thoughtful expression in his eyes caused her to ask, "What is it?"

"You're becoming an important part of my life."

The words caressed her.

"That's not supposed to make you cry."

She swiped at her sudden tears. Emotion turned her bones to sand. She made an effort to stiffen her legs.

He bent his head. Anticipating his kiss, she parted her lips. When he touched his mouth to hers, she knew an overwhelming sense of rightness. He smelled of soap and leather.

"This could become a habit," he said when he lifted his head.

His words had her cheeks heating with color.

She thought she understood what the admission had cost him. A man like Ford wouldn't be comfortable showing vulnerability.

For her own peace of mind, she needed to put some space between them and took a step back.

He must have sensed her feelings, for he didn't press her.

She dared not dream about a future with him. Right now, she needed time to think, and that was impossible while she remained in the warm circle of Ford's arms.

She didn't try to hide the trembling that his kiss had produced and was thankful for his understanding. She was sorry to see the day come to a close and said as much.

Lavender shadows darkened to a deep purple as they rode over the open plain. They returned to town as dusk settled, the stars pinpricks in the darkening sky.

"Sam always said that stars were holes in the curtain of the night." Sam hadn't been much with words, but he had found a way of using nature to describe his feelings. "We used to make wishes on them." She missed him with a terrible longing that went straight to her heart.

The day had been as perfect as any day she could remember. She tried not to think of the significance of that perfection.

What she had with Ford was too new, too fragile, to analyze.

"Something wrong?" he asked, that quicksilver smile of his nearly destroying her ability to think altogether.

"N . . . nothing." Everything. Her world had just been turned upside down. She wondered if he had an inkling of what she was thinking. Feeling.

Ford hadn't slept worth a darn, thanks to a certain russet-haired reporter and kisses that had shaken him more than he cared to admit. He wanted to blame his unaccustomed behavior on a full moon, but the sky had been an unbroken strip of indigo.

The familiar scent of horseflesh, along with the

soft nuzzling from Frosty's nose, brought him back to reality.

The horses blew an occasional greeting and munched contentedly on straw.

He swept the barn until the floor was as clean as the wood floor in his mama's kitchen. The horses needed clean stalls. He wondered what it said about him that he was meticulous about where he kept his animals but was indifferent to his own comfort.

The rented house was nothing to boast about. He'd taken it because it was close to town. He'd ignored the house, concentrating on fixing up the barn. More often than not he bunked at the jail.

Hawk had been with him for five years. He'd picked up Frosty, a sweet little mare, when he moved to Colorado Springs. She was company for the gelding, her gentle disposition a foil to the more high-spirited Hawk.

After seeing to the horses, he wandered outside.

He stared at where the plain lay blue-gray like a morning sea against a distant horizon. A dazzling streak at first, but growing rapidly, the sun wheeled above the fuzzy line. Its rays only hinted at the heat that would soon blanket the land. For now, it warmed him and cast a pleasant glow over the outbuildings. Not even its radiance could disguise the run-down condition of the place, though.

With Cady at his side, Ford was accepted into the town's heart. With reserve, to be sure, but accepted nonetheless. The postmistress addressed him by name, rather than the formal title of *Sheriff*. Doris Conway served him up a smile along with his morning coffee at the cafe.

He recalled Cady's simple use of the word *home*. It was that that he'd been searching for, without even knowing it.

He savored the feeling of knowing that he belonged, however temporarily. He didn't delude himself that it was he, Ford McKinnon, who had been embraced by the town; it was Cady's beau who had been approved.

It was, he told himself, enough. Belonging was belonging. He'd known too little of it to reject it, no matter what its source.

More and more often Cady fell comfortably into his thoughts. He felt a smile slide into place. There was no denying the spring in his step or the anticipation he felt upon waking in the morning. He thought of the evening of the town dance, the pleasure he'd taken in simply being with her.

A few months ago, just the thought of something like that would have had him running in the other direction. He had rarely taken the time to experience the sweet enjoyment of simply being with a pretty woman. Instead, the more he was with Cady, the more he longed to be with her. There was something in this woman that he recognized in himself.

Ford didn't know what to make of his feelings.

They were completely different than any he had ever experienced. This wasn't the simple physical attraction of a man for a comely woman. It was more. Much more.

And it was as unsettling as the woman herself.

Chapter Seven

Another ranch had been hit. Unfortunately for Ford, it was the mayor's place.

Mayor Gardner glowered at Ford. "Took your own sweet time getting here. I've got chores that need doing and a town that needs running. I can't just sit on my rump waiting for you to show up."

"I came as soon as I got word," Ford said mildly.

Gardner snorted. "You promised us results. Now it's my spread. You think I can afford to lose a hundred and fifty head?"

Ford took a firm grip on his patience and prayed that it held. "No, sir. I don't. I promised you I'd put a stop to the rustling, and I aim to do just that. I suggest you get on with your work and let me get on with mine."

"I pulled all but two of my men over to the east pasture," Gardner said, ignoring Ford's hint that he take himself off. "How did they know where to hit?"

Ford wondered the same thing. He didn't like the answer he kept coming up with. The rustlers were local, likely men he'd met, talked with, shared drinks with at the saloon. Heck, they might even work for Gardner or one of the other ranchers.

He cupped a hand over his brow, letting his gaze scan the Gardner spread. The straggly fields, run-down fences, and unpainted outbuildings, all were mute testament to the mayor's penny-pinching ways.

Ford did what he could—checked the west pasture where the cattle had been grazing and looked for tracks. The ground was baked hard by the late-summer sun, unwilling to give up many of its secrets. What tracks he found could have belonged to anyone, including the mayor himself.

He returned to town, more discouraged than he wanted to admit. He spent the next days questioning everyone who had visited the Gardner ranch recently, up to and including the town reverend, who had been soliciting donations for the church's building fund.

That pious man had taken offense and complained to the mayor's wife, who then complained to her husband.

Ford had received a summons to the mayor's office and left with his ears ringing.

"Questioning the reverend? Is that what you call

doing your job?" Gardner had demanded. "I don't have to tell you that Mrs. Gardner gave me an earful about it. Don't know why she invited that old fussbudget to the ranch anyway. He doesn't do anything but preach forgiveness and ask for money. That's all anyone wants. Money!" He clucked like an overwrought hen. "I'm not made of the stuff."

Ford tucked his tongue into one cheek. The mayor might boss the town, but it was clear who bossed the mayor.

Efforts to trace the missing cattle by brand had failed to bring any answers. Telegrams to sheriffs in neighboring towns had produced the same results.

Ford decided to pay a visit to the saloon. Nothing went on in the town or county that didn't get talked about at the local watering hole.

He timed his visit carefully. Daytime hours, especially those in the morning, were usually quiet. What he had to say, he wanted to say in private.

Charlie Flynn, proprietor and bartender, raised an eyebrow as Ford swung open the flimsy doors. "Haven't seen you in here since the boys got rowdy last payday."

Boot heels clicking on the straw-strewn floor, Ford crossed the room, slid onto a bar stool, and hooked his heels on its rungs. "I need some information."

Flynn continued drying glasses. "What kind?"

"Who's got money they shouldn't. Who's bragging and who's keeping quiet."

Flynn scratched his head. "I don't pay no attention to gossip."

That earned a snort from Ford. "You hear more than all the gossips put together. All I'm asking is that you tell me about anything that sounds a bit off. Anything at all."

Flynn cocked an eyebrow. "What's in it for me?"

Ford had expected that and was prepared. "Use your head. If the ranchers keep losing stock, they're gonna sell out. The ranchers move out, businesses will close up. No one's gonna have money to spend here. Or anywhere else." He let that sink in.

Flynn lined up glasses on a shelf, then turned back to Ford. He scratched his bearded chin, considering. "All you want is for me to keep my eyes and ears open. That it?"

"That's it." Ford sketched a salute in parting, praying that his trust wasn't misplaced. It was possible that Flynn could tip off the rustlers.

Years of sheriffing made a man think twice before trusting anyone. Ford had made a decision to trust Flynn.

Two days later, he got a message to come to the saloon. Flynn had come through. He passed a slip of paper to Ford.

"Thanks," Ford said after reading the two-word message. "I owe you one." None of the excitement racing through his blood was reflected in his voice.

Ford wasn't particularly surprised at the names.

He'd had his suspicions but no proof. With what Flynn had given him, he ought to have that within a day, two at the most.

The pieces fell into place at last.

Jeb Lassiter liked the good life, sitting in the saloon and buying a round of drinks, buying cheap dresses and cheaper perfume for the fancy girls who worked there. He liked to pull out a wad of money from his pocket and watch his friends' eyes glaze over, their mouths fall open. Money didn't just slip through his fingers. It poured as though from a cracked dam.

At one time or another Jeb had hired on as an extra hand for all of the ranches that had been hit. He knew every square inch of land, every box canyon, every way in and out. What better place to conceal stolen cattle than the canyons that gutted the land?

Ford held out his hand. "Thanks."

After a moment's pause, Flynn took it. "We square?"

"You need a favor, you know where to look."

"You'll be doing me—heck, the whole town—a favor if you bring in those varmints."

Preoccupied with what he'd learned, Ford returned to the jail, nearly running into Sonny as the boy swept the office.

"Sorry, Sheriff."

"My fault," Ford said.

In the past weeks, Sonny had shown up every day, eager to do whatever chore Ford assigned, including sweeping the office and scrubbing out the cells. It was no mean job, emptying the privy buckets and swabbing the floors stained by tobacco juice and food.

The boy had a natural curiosity and peppered Ford with questions whenever he could.

Sonny looked up at Ford with wide-eyed interest. "I heard you was over at the saloon."

So much for secrecy, Ford thought. "That's right."

"Looking for clues about the rustlers, I bet," the boy added, his breath gusting with excitement. He was all but jumping up and down.

Ford rubbed a hand over Sonny's head. Unbidden, a grin escaped his lips. The rustlers were still Sonny's main topic of conversation. Had he ever been that young? "Finish up the sweeping, and you can take off."

"I don't mind sticking around if'n you got some more chores for me," Sonny said.

"Your ma and pa will be looking for you."

" 'kay, Sheriff."

Ford's grin vanished as he thought of what lay ahead. Contrary to what Sonny thought, he didn't look forward to hunting down men, possibly having to draw down on them. How could he?

Cady looked up as the door swung open.

Ford stood there, his shoulders brushing the splintered wood frame. It wasn't just his size that seemed to dominate the room. It was an aura he transmitted, one of power, strength, and assurance.

The room seemed to shrink, his presence eating up the until-now adequate space. Just the sight of him sparked a ripple of happiness in her.

It faded as she took in the hard line of his mouth, the flat look in his eyes. Her brow furrowed, and a sickening certainty knotted her stomach. He was going after the rustlers.

With a single stride, he stood so close that she wasn't sure whose heartbeat she heard—his or her own. Her pulse picked up its beat, the blood pounding in her ears. The breath died in her throat.

She swallowed. Hard.

He took her hand and turned it over to press a kiss into the center of her palm. The tremor that shuddered through her was out of proportion to the simple gesture.

He cupped a hand under her elbow and urged her to the storeroom. "I have a lead on the rustlers."

A small, hot breeze from the tiny window stirred the air, but she felt a chill tremble down her arm. She recognized the source. Fear. For him.

"Alone?" She prayed he'd take Robb Turner with him.

"Yeah." There was no give in the single word. "Robb's green. I don't want him anywhere near it."

There was a twist in her gut, one quick churn that

had her praying the meat loaf she'd had at the cafe didn't back up on her. "What about you?"

A half smile touched his lips. "I've been taking care of myself for a long time."

Her gut stayed all pinched up. "That doesn't make you invincible."

He pulled her to him. "I'll be all right."

Words sprang to her lips, warning him not to take chances, to wait until he could round up more men. She swallowed them back.

He would hear the fear in them, and it would hurt him. More, it might distract him from what he had to do.

She knew that all the words, the holding him in her arms, the feelings she had for him would not change the reality he had to face. She ignored her fluttery heartbeat and concentrated on his face.

"Don't let the bad guys get the jump on you." She was joking to hide the wrenching worry that gnawed at her.

She felt a jolt of fear, the same jolt she'd experienced every time Sam had strapped on a gun. She hadn't been able to stop him. She wouldn't be able to stop Ford. And even if she could, she wouldn't.

He slipped his arms around her waist.

She melted into his embrace and forgot the fear, forgot everything but the feel of her arms around him and the touch of her lips against his.

"You'll be careful." Her voice, she was proud to note, was steady.

"Is that concern I hear?" The smile in his voice was nearly her undoing and had her closing her eyes.

"I was a lawman's daughter." And she didn't know if she wanted to be a lawman's wife. She reminded herself that the question hadn't come up. If it did, she didn't know what her answer would be.

"Be safe."

"You can count on it." He slanted his mouth over hers and kissed her. "I'll be back."

She took comfort from the quiet assurance in his voice. She walked with him to the door.

"What's wrong?" Emilie asked after Ford had left.

Cady gave a terse explanation.

"You're worried about him." Emilie's flat statement left no room for argument.

"He knows how to take care of himself." The words were said more to herself than to her friend.

"Of course he does. He's a good lawman. Just like Sam." Emilie laid a hand on Cady's. "He'll be careful. And he'll be back."

Cady smiled at her friend in gratitude. She kept busy, too busy to worry. Or so she told herself. But she couldn't quiet the uneasiness that filled her. Feathers of fear whispered down her spine.

She tamped down the worry as best she could.

When she couldn't fight it any longer, she slumped over her desk, head pillowed on her arms.

She thought of Ford facing rustlers alone. *Let him be safe,* she prayed silently. She closed up the paper, then walked outside to her buggy and headed home. At the cabin, she heated up some leftover stew, pushed it around on her plate, then carefully covered it with a cloth. She extinguished the oil lamp and crawled into bed.

She thrashed about the bed, battling a dozen warring emotions. Finally, she drifted into sleep, then awoke hours later with the clammy sweat of fear clinging to her. In her dream, she saw Ford, covered with blood, his face contorted in pain. She tried to reach him but couldn't, her efforts hampered by swirling mists of darkness.

Breath sawing, she clawed her way out of the nightmare. That's all it was, she told herself. A nightmare. Ford was too savvy, too experienced, to allow himself to be ambushed.

Being a lawman wasn't just a job. It was a way of life, one that demanded total commitment, not only from the man himself but from those who loved him. She'd shared Sam, not with brothers and sisters, but with the whole town.

She'd never questioned the way of things, accepting it because she'd loved him.

Love had made the difference.

That startled her. She couldn't seem to grab a breath of air.

Did she love Ford? How did she know? Was it the thump of her heart when he was near? Or the sweet joy that thrummed through her when he kissed her? Or maybe it was as simple as knowing she was a better person when she was with him.

She had no experience with romantic love, with the heady excitement penny novels described. She only knew that being with him felt right. Very, very right.

Ford touched his heels to Hawk's flanks.

Hawk shifted impatiently beneath him. The wind picked up, pricking his face with sand. His hat nearly blew off before he caught it and tilted it lower.

The crimson light of the setting sun reminded him of another ride, one shared with Cady.

This was not the time to think about Cady. When he found the rustlers, he'd need a hundred percent of his concentration focused on them.

With the discipline that defined every part of his life, he was already working on tucking her into a back corner of his mind.

They climbed higher. The air had thinned. Hawk whickered in response to the change in the atmosphere. The terrain had changed accordingly, the ground becoming rougher, the stands of pines growing thicker until the dense green appeared almost black.

Within another month, two at the most, the aspen would turn gold, their brightness all the shinier against the near black of the pine, a last hurrah of color against the stark whiteness of winter.

He stopped for the night. A puny breeze cooled his skin. Soon enough it would turn to a cold wind. The dry mountain air had a bite to it, even in late summer.

The high country held its own beauty, one that couldn't be dismissed or denied. Just as potent were its dangers. A man would be a fool to ignore them.

After giving Hawk food and water, he caught a rabbit in a snare and roasted it over a spit, careful to keep the fire low. The meat was stringy, but it filled the hole in his gut, and that was the most important thing.

He doused the fire, then undid his bedroll. It wasn't the first night he'd spent under the sky. It wouldn't be the last. He climbed into the bedroll, grateful for its warmth against the increasing cold.

The night was fierce with stars, each so sharply cut that it appeared to be a chunk of fool's gold against the black canopy of the sky.

Night sounds gathered around him—the cry of a coyote, the hoot of an owl—all as familiar as his own heartbeat. He went to sleep with the quiet thrum of the wind echoing off the canyon walls.

The sky was hard dark when he woke. He saw to Hawk, then breakfasted on dried beef and hardtack washed down with a trickle of water.

Ford had hunted for years. He knew how to bide his time while his quarry exhausted itself. Fresh tracks had him slowing his pace while he planned his strategy.

This time his quarry was two-legged and a lot more canny than a cougar or a bear. And this time he didn't have the luxury of patience. Time was running out.

The sun was merciless, and he adjusted the angle of his hat to shade more of his face. He struggled to ignore the light sweat of fear that had dried on his skin and felt the hair spike on the back of his neck.

He was getting closer.

His breathing grew shallow, and he knew it wasn't due solely to the thinness of the air. He recognized the signs of his body readying for what lay ahead. He'd been a lawman for too many years to dismiss the danger he faced.

Long ago he'd accepted that he wasn't invincible. A man didn't last long in his chosen profession if he allowed himself to believe that he was.

Abruptly, danger snapped into the air. He felt it— the tingling of nerves, the stillness that didn't feel right. His skin prickled with awareness, and sweat gathered on his neck beneath his Stetson.

The ground dropped off into a narrow canyon all but hidden from view. If he hadn't been looking for it, he'd have missed the entrance to the gulley altogether.

Ford dismounted and edged closer, his booted feet

making no noise on the uneven ground. Years of tracking prey, both the two-footed and the four-footed kind, had taught him to move silently.

Smell came first—the pungent, unmistakable scent of cattle crowded together and a foul, burned smell. Branding. The rustlers were changing the brands.

There was something under that, something metallic. He sniffed again. Blood. Fresh blood. The scent was unmistakable. Jeb and Howie had probably butchered a steer or two for their own use.

Then came the sounds, the gentle lowing that he normally found soothing. Now, it sounded eerie, a backdrop to a menacing setting.

Like a deer who scented danger, he came to attention, every muscle taut. He recognized the edginess in his hands, the readiness in his legs, the tension in his shoulders. Nerves skated up his spine but were ruthlessly shaken off.

Ford was accustomed to watching and waiting for openings. Trained hunters learned those skills early on or ended up unemployed. Or dead.

Jeb Lassiter and Howie Marlow were branding a young steer. The smell of seared flesh now overrode everything else, including blood. So intent were they on their task that they didn't notice Ford's approach.

He leveled his rifle. "It's over, Jeb, Howie." Slowly, deliberately, he cocked the trigger.

A creak of leather signaled that Jeb had shifted his weight, bracing himself.

Ford watched the twitch of Jeb's cheek, the slight shift in his shoulders. Ford widened his stance, his gaze never leaving the rustlers. "Don't," he said, allowing the one word to make the statement.

"For Pete's sake, don't shoot," Howie said, his Adam's apple bobbling. Sweat was popping out on his forehead.

"Unholster your guns, boys. Place them on the ground. Real slow. Now kick them away."

After the men dropped their weapons, Ford picked them up and tucked them at the small of his back.

He tossed Jeb a length of rope. "Tie Howie's hands behind his back. And make it nice and tight."

When Howie was secured, Ford did the same with Jeb. He tested the rope on both men's hands.

"You can't take us back," Jeb said, voice rising to a pleading whine. "Let us go, and I promise we'll hightail it out of here. You'll never hear from us again."

Ford shook his head. "You know I can't do that."

"Why?"

"I took an oath. It's my job to bring you in." And for Ford, that said it all.

Jeb spat. "Your job. Do you know what they'll do to us in the state prison?"

Ford smothered a ripple of sympathy because he did know. "Maybe you should have thought of that before you started stealing from the folks around here."

"We didn't rightly think it through."

He believed that. Neither Jeb nor Howie was long on brains. He turned to put the guns into his saddle-bag and felt more than saw the movement on Jeb's part.

Before he could turn, Jeb head-butted him, Howie rushing in to shoulder him to the ground. Even with their hands tied, the men managed to put up a good fight.

Ford yanked Howie down and held him with an elbow to the windpipe. Ignoring Howie's squeal of pain, Ford slammed a fist into Jeb's middle.

Jeb groaned, turned onto his side, and heaved.

The trip back to town was anticlimactic after that as Jeb and Howie griped the entire time, complaining that the ropes were too tight and blaming each other for the whole thing.

"I told you to keep your money in your pocket 'til everything died down," Howie muttered to Jeb.

"Keep your mouth shut," Jeb ordered.

It made sense now. The fight in the saloon a few weeks ago. They must have been arguing over Jeb's need to play the big man and spread around a little too much extra cash.

By the time they reached town, Ford was bone-weary, his muscles weeping with fatigue. He yawned so hard, his jaw popped.

The thought of a bath and bed, not necessarily in that order, had kept him going. That and the prospect of seeing Cady. His entire body softened as he brought up a picture of her in his mind.

He settled his prisoners in jail, cleaned up, and went to find Cady. He wasn't surprised to see a light glowing at the *Gazette.*

Softly, he pushed open the door and found her slumped at her desk, head pillowed on her folded arms.

He became aware of the sense of connection that came when he saw her. It calmed him and gave him a centered feeling that he couldn't explain.

He let his gaze rest on the woman who was fast becoming the most important thing in his life. A woman who was every bit as appealing in the bright light of day as she was by moonlight. A woman who gave comfort as easily as she breathed.

She lifted her head, her eyes widening with undisguised pleasure when they registered his presence.

"It's done."

She ran to him and closed her arms around him.

He felt her every shift and sigh, the trembling of her hands as they ran over him, as though to assure herself that he was all right.

"You're safe. I hoped . . . prayed you would be."

He took her hands in his and brought them to his lips. When was the last time anyone had prayed for him? Not since his mother died.

There was more he wanted to say to her, but it was late. They were both tired.

He saw the shadows under her eyes. "You should be at home. In bed."

Cady didn't play games. Her eyes, as honest as every other part of her, met his in a steady gaze. "I couldn't leave until I knew you were all right."

Chapter Eight

Talk of Ford's catching the rustlers hummed through the ladies' quilting bee and displaced the news that one of the church elders had actually sworn during the Wednesday prayer meeting.

In the way of small towns, unofficial reports outstripped official ones as curiosity and excitement fanned the gossip to a wildfire. Everyone had had time to form an opinion.

"I heard the sheriff darn near took off Jeb's arm with a bowie knife," one rancher told another at Doris' cafe.

"I got the lowdown from the boy who delivers the food to the prisoners," the second man put in. "He said that Ford held Howie facedown over an open fire just for fun."

Doris shook her head. "You two don't know Ford if you believe that."

All this was reported to Ford by Robb, who was nearly as disappointed as Sonny with the unexciting truth.

In one account, Ford heard that he had threatened to gut-shoot Jeb when he refused to drop his gun. Another had Ford using his bare hands to bring down the rustlers. He knew the truth, knew it was tame by comparison.

And was thankful for it.

No lawman, no *real* lawman, wanted to maim or kill another human being. The memory of having to kill a man three years ago still burned within his mind. And his gut.

He had done what he'd had to to protect his town, his people, but he knew he would never forget the pain that ricocheted through him at the knowledge that he'd taken a life.

He had brought in Jeb and Howie. No guns or knives had been used. No heroics had been involved.

"Go to the saloon," he ordered Sonny. "See if you can round up four men looking to earn a few dollars to bring in the cattle."

Sonny returned within the hour, four cowpokes trailing behind.

"What you planning to pay, Sheriff?" one asked.

"Deputy's salary," Ford said, with a wince at the mayor's probable reaction to that.

"They say you didn't have to fire a shot," another said, the avid gleam in his eyes making it clear he'd hoped for another story.

"They say right."

Ford didn't blame everyone for wanting a more sensational version of the events, but he wasn't about to apologize that he couldn't provide it.

"That's all?" Sonny asked, obviously disappointed when Ford told him the real story.

"That's all." Ford tucked his tongue into one cheek. The boy's case of hero worship had plummeted, and Ford could only be grateful for that.

The last thing an impressionable boy needed was to pin his sights on a man who made his living with a gun. Much better that he look to his pa for an example of what a man was supposed to be. Lars Henriksen provided for his family, doing backbreaking work every day of the week. In Ford's book, that took real courage.

Sonny's crestfallen face prompted Ford to suggest, "Why don't you take off early today? I hear your pa has a new foal. Likely as not, he could use some help with her."

"Could I?"

Ford grinned. The lure of a foal outweighed the tame story of his bringing in the rustlers. "Get going before I change my mind."

The boy took off, then turned. "Thanks, Sheriff."

Manners, Ford thought. Sonny's folks had taught

their boy well. His own ma had tried to teach Ford the same. He wondered how his life would have been different had she lived.

Time to question his prisoners. He unlocked the door separating the office from the cells. The stench of unwashed bodies and stale air filled the small cell area. He spared a moment to picture what Jeb and Howie faced. Pity stirred within him.

By state prison standards, the cell was a palace. Each man had a bunk. Each had a privy bucket. Each was fed three squares a day.

There were no beatings, no backbreaking labor, no leg irons. He knew enough of what went on in the state prison to not wish a stretch there upon his worst enemy.

Still, the men had stolen from their neighbors, stolen the only means many of the townspeople had to make a living. He couldn't let pity prevent him from doing his duty.

Ford leaned against the stone wall of the jail and looked at Lassister. It hadn't taken long to determine that he was the boss of the rustling duo. Jeb was sly, and Howie was definitely short in the brains department.

Both men threw Ford bitter looks.

He didn't take it personally. He figured they were entitled to feel a mite annoyed with him. "You're looking at hard time."

"I got me something to trade." Lassister tucked a

wad of chaw inside his cheek. "It weren't just Howie and me what was doing the rustling."

So, there'd been a third man. Ford wasn't surprised. The rustling had been smooth, too organized, to be only a two-man operation.

"You want to give me a name?"

Lassiter took a moment to noisily chew the tobacco, then spat a nasty-looking stream at the far wall. "What you want to give me for it?"

"I don't have the power to give you anything at all. That's up to the prosecutor and the judge."

A humming silence, broken only by Jeb's incessant chewing, stretched.

"Maybe I don't want to deal with them. Maybe I want to deal with you." His face creased in a knife-edged grin.

Ford feigned disinterest. "Your choice."

"Sam Armstrong."

Ford snorted. "You expect me to believe that Sheriff Sam Armstrong was in on the rustling? If brains were leather, Jeb, you couldn't saddle a bug."

"That right? How do you think we got away with it for so many months? Armstrong made sure the posse never got near us."

"Armstrong was as honest as they come. He wouldn't take a bribe." Still, an uneasy feeling worked its way up Ford's throat. Hadn't he, himself, wondered why Sam hadn't caught the rustlers?

"It weren't no bribe. Sam took part of the loot.

Heck, he caught us before the first month was out. Was ready to haul us in. That's when I got the idea to cut him in. He wanted money for that gal of his."

"Cady?"

"He knowed he didn't have much longer to live. He wanted to leave her something."

Ford let his skepticism show. "You got any proof?"

"Why would I lie?"

"To buy yourself a lesser sentence."

"Take a look at the sheriff's bankbook. See what he's got stashed away."

Ford wanted to forget the whole thing. What did it matter? Armstrong was dead. He'd seen lawmen go bad. Unfortunately, it wasn't all that uncommon. Sheriffs, even the best ones, worked for a dollar a day. They bought their own bullets, paid for their own room and board. It didn't leave much to spare.

But Sam Armstrong was a legend. Ford only hoped that the legend wasn't tarnished. Not for Sam's sake— the dead man was beyond caring. But for Cady's. She worshipped her father.

Jeb slanted an insolent look in Ford's direction. "I want to talk to Sam's gal."

Ford's response was automatic. "Stay away from Cady."

Jeb gave a satisfied nod. "So, that's the way it is."

"She doesn't have anything to do with this."

"Do you want her to hear it around town?"

Jeb had a point. Once the story was out—and Ford knew it would get out—there was no way she wouldn't hear about it.

Life offered hard choices sometimes. His brain said one thing, but his heart, the part that belonged to Cady, said another. Duty required that he find the truth.

If he didn't perform his duty, if he acted without honor, he had nothing.

He had little in the way of material goods. Two horses. A saddle. A gun. His integrity was about all he had to offer. To himself. To anyone.

He reviewed his choices. He could resign as sheriff. Under the constant threat of danger and everyday annoyances, though, lurked the absolute certainty that he was part of something important. He never talked about it. No lawman worth his salt did.

It was there, though, buried deep inside, the awareness that he was playing his own small part in building a great country. Sheriffing was all he'd ever done, all he'd ever wanted to do.

That was why he risked his life every time he strapped on a gun. That was why he put in twelve-hour days seven days a week for little more than room and board. That was why he wouldn't ignore Jeb's charge, no matter how much he might want to.

What about Cady? What happens if Jeb isn't lying? What will it do to her?

He was sure of only one thing: whatever the truth

was, Cady had a right to hear it before it became common knowledge.

He would check it out. He had to. He owed Sam Armstrong that. He owed Cady.

When he walked into the *Gazette* office, Cady looked up and smiled. He wanted to keep that smile on her face for the rest of his life. Yet he knew he was destined to destroy it.

Cady felt a nervous fluttering of her heart. The knowing look Emilie sent her way told her that her assistant recognized what she was feeling. And why.

Ford didn't return the smile Cady sent his way. "Cady." Something in his voice snagged her attention, something shading toward regret. "Our star boarder wants to see you."

"Does he want me to do a story about him?"

"No." Tension angled his shoulders.

Her professional instincts homed in on the emphasis on the single word. "What's wrong?"

Ford shook his head. "I think you'd better hear it for yourself." His voice was husky, labored, as if he were pulling it from someplace deep inside him.

"All right." She wiped the worst of the ink from her hands.

They made the short trip to the jail, the silence stretching between them. She glanced at Ford and wondered what had dug grooves into his forehead and pulled his lips taut.

Ford ushered her into the sheriff's office. She

wanted to question him, to ask what had put the shadows into his eyes. The closed expression on his face stopped her. A sense of foreboding skittered through her, and a knot formed in her stomach.

He unlocked the iron door to the cell area.

Jeb Lassiter was chewing on a piece of straw. Something in his eyes had her pausing. She frowned as she tried to identify what it was. Triumph.

That was ridiculous. Jeb was going to serve hard time, and he knew it. She felt a stirring of pity for him as she recalled stories she'd heard of life in the state prison.

She braced her hands on her hips. "You wanted to see me?"

"Yeah. We got us some jawing to do."

"Do you want me to write your story in the paper?" It wouldn't be the first time an outlaw had wanted to see his name in print.

"You could say that," he said in a laconic tone.

"Look, Jeb, you got something to say, say it. Otherwise, I've got a paper to get out."

Jeb smirked. "You want to know the truth about the rustling? How we was able to keep it going without your pa catching on?"

She nodded.

"We didn't."

It took a moment for the significance of the words to penetrate. She didn't believe it. Not for a moment. She turned and headed to the door.

Jeb's next words caused her to stop. "You afraid to hear the truth about your pa? About how he turned a blind eye to what we was doing?"

"You're lying."

"You sure about that?"

"I'm sure." But her voice lacked conviction. She was remembering the money that had arrived unexpectedly when she was apprenticing in Boston. Sam had dismissed her concern when she'd asked about it, saying he'd gotten a bonus from the town council. Now she wondered.

Jeb had planted a seed of doubt. She hated him for that. More, she hated herself for letting him. The knot in her stomach jerked tighter.

"Are you?" Jeb let the two words hang in the ensuing silence.

She turned and looked at the man who sprawled on the cot, his belly spilling out of a ripped shirt. She schooled her voice to one of disinterest, even while a chill flowed through her. "Why don't you tell me how Sam came to be involved?"

"It was like this, see. Howie and me had this setup. A man up in Denver had the connections to move the cattle without attracting notice. All we had to do was supply him." Jeb cackled. "Sort of supply and demand, you know?

"Anyways, we started up, only your pa caught on right away. He was plenty smart. Only he was greedy. Cut himself in on the whole operation. Had some notion of paying off the note on his place." He gave her a sly look. "Can't blame him. Did it for you, girl, he did."

Cady told herself that the word of a confessed rustler was nothing to worry about. She laughed, not with humor but frayed nerves. "I don't have to step in manure to know when I'm on a horse track. And I don't have to stand in it to know when I'm talking to a no-account drifter who'd like nothing better than to smear a good man's name."

Still, she couldn't help but recall the beaten look on Sam's face when she'd last seen him. She'd chalked it up to his failure to put an end to the rustling. Now she wondered. Had it been failure . . . or guilt?

She pushed the thought aside. Sam had been a lawman for all of his adult life. He had lived for the job, loved it just as he did the town. He would never betray the people he'd sworn to protect.

She looked down and saw that her fingers were clenched so tightly around the bars, her knuckles had whitened under the pressure. Carefully, one by one, she undid each. At the same time, she worked to quiet the jumpy feeling in her gut.

"What made you think you could trust Sam? He could have been stringing you along, giving you enough rope to hang yourself." She desperately wanted to believe that.

Jeb gave an ugly smile. "If you can't trust greed, what can you trust?"

She drew a breath of relief and knew that Jeb was lying. Sam hadn't had a greedy bone in him.

The breath snagged in her throat, though, as questions teased her brain. Where *had* the extra money come from? And why had Sam, who had never before kept a secret from her, suddenly turned close-mouthed?

With an effort, she swallowed the lump in her throat and found her voice. "I know the truth. What kind of man tries to ruin a good man's reputation just for spite?"

"I don't hold it against your pa." Jeb shrugged. "I'm gonna do time. I figure I might get a couple of years off if I come clean."

All the more reason for him to lie.

"I'm not listening to any more of your lies." She turned her attention to Howie, who occupied the neighboring cell. "What do you have to say?"

Howie tugged at his shirt collar. "It were like Jeb said. Your pa was in on it."

Unlike Jeb, Howie didn't seem to take pleasure in saying the words.

She rapped on the door.

Ford opened it, his expression wary. She could only stare at him as tension filled the dim interior of the jail in a suffocating blanket of silence.

She shot him a look of sheer resentment. "You knew what he was going to tell me."

"Yeah."

She began to pace, her feet tracing a path on the dusty wood floor, her body stiff with hostility.

A muscle worked overtime in the corner of Ford's jaw as he watched her.

"Jeb's word is hardly proof," she said.

His nod was a curt acknowledgment, but something like sorrow flickered in his eyes.

She needed to move, to work off the anger, but she discovered that her knees were shaking.

He pulled out a chair and gestured for her to sit.

She sat and folded her arms across her chest, a defensive measure. She took a moment to gather her thoughts. "Is that why you didn't stay?" She scarcely recognized the voice as her own, so flat and cold was it.

"Figured you had a right to hear it without an audience."

She might have appreciated his sensitivity if the fury bubbling inside her hadn't overridden everything else. She tamped it down and placed a hand on his arm. "Can't you see that Jeb is lying? He's had a grudge against my father for as long as I can remember. He'd do anything to hurt Sam. Even after he's dead."

It wasn't possible, she told herself. Jeb didn't like Sam, so he'd made up a story to blacken his reputation.

That was it. Jeb wanted to pay Sam back for when he'd evicted Jeb's father for failure to pay back taxes.

She latched on to the explanation with all the fervor that fear had produced.

She remembered Sam's grief over having to force a family from their home, but the bank had sold the house, leaving Sam no other choice. Sam had tried to help Jeb's father find a job, but the man had taken to the bottle instead. Jeb had been only a boy then, a sullen boy who had grown more sullen as the years passed.

The explanation settled her queasy stomach. If Jeb's story were true, everything she thought she knew was a lie.

"What are you going to do?" It was hard, brutally hard, to ask, but she had to know.

Ford stood there, his bearing as straight and certain as honor. "I have to investigate." His eyes turned bleak. "If I had a choice, I'd forget the whole thing. But I don't."

"I know."

Of course he had to find the truth. His moral code wouldn't allow anything else. It was only one of the things she admired about him. But how could she feel what she did for the man who was determined to prove her father guilty of rustling? She knew she was being unfair but was powerless to stop her feelings.

"Do what you have to do. But don't expect me to believe that Sam had anything to do with the rustling."

She pushed back the chair and stood. "You'd like to prove it, wouldn't you? To show Sam up. To show everyone around here that the great Sam Armstrong had feet of clay. Because that's the only way you'll be accepted," she ended, her voice spiny with bitterness. She threw him a hard look. "You want Jeb to be right, don't you?"

His rugged face never changed expression, but his eyes now wore a shuttered look, and his voice went cold. "I want the truth."

So did she. Or she thought she did.

He reached for her, only to drop his hand when she backed away. "I'm sorry, Cady did."

"Don't. Don't call me that."

"Because that was his name for you?"

"Because I don't know what I feel. Not now."

"Don't make me choose," he said at last.

"Don't make me." She turned away, head high, back painfully straight. "I'm going home." If the answers were anywhere, she'd find them there.

Fighting tears and cursing herself for even entertaining the idea that Jeb was telling the truth, she pushed open the door and let herself out into the blinding Colorado sunshine.

Once outside, she let her shoulders slump.

Abruptly, she stiffened them. She had nothing for which to apologize. Not for Sam. Not for herself.

Anger and fear pushed her past the *Gazette* office, past Emilie's frantic wave, to the livery stable where she kept her rig during the day.

Ford watched her progress down the road. He

wanted to follow her, to make sure she reached home all right. His throat burned with all that he couldn't say, couldn't do, couldn't change.

She shouldn't be by herself. She should have a friend with her. He started after her, but good sense kicked in. He laughed, a harsh sound that held no humor. He was the last person Cady wanted near her. He couldn't even offer the prickly comfort of his presence.

Her last words had lashed him with stinging stripes. He knew frustration was at the source of her anger, but the fact that he'd been caught in its path hurt, hurt more than he'd thought possible.

Was it true? he wondered. Did he want to prove that Sam Armstrong had fallen? It shamed him that she might be right. He'd spent months in Colorado Springs trying to measure up to a legend and knowing he never would.

What she said made sense. But he couldn't shake the uneasy feeling that there was more to Lassiter's words than simple meanness.

Ford scrubbed a hand through his hair. He couldn't continue his investigation without hurting Cady, and he couldn't do his job without investigating.

Never let the job become personal. That advice had been hammered into him from the first day he pinned on a badge. This was the first time he'd seriously doubted his ability to follow it.

His sigh came on a wave of resignation. Duty came first. It always had.

Because he was a lawman.

Because he had taken an oath to uphold the law.

Because he had given his word to the people of Colorado Springs.

There were few things a man could count on in this world. He liked to think his word was one of them.

The idea that Sam Armstrong had been part of the rustling felt as if someone had yanked a good hunk of the earth out from under his feet.

He stalked back to the cell and eyed Lassiter. Raw anger roughened his voice. "You're going to have to give me a lot more than your word that Sam Armstrong was involved in the rustling."

Jeb leaned back, an insolent smile on his face. "I can give you dates and places. You check 'em out, then tell me I'm lying."

Ford reminded himself that Sam Armstrong was a lawman's lawman. His own doubts bubbled again. A little harder. A little longer.

He listened as Jeb recounted a list of dates and places, how Sam had made sure he and the posse were far away from the spreads Jeb and Howie planned to hit.

"I'll check out your stories," Ford said. That was all he said, all he could say.

Wearily, he returned to his desk. He massaged the back of his neck in a futile attempt to loosen the knot that had settled between his shoulder blades.

If he buried what Jeb had told him, he'd protect Sam Armstrong's name. More, he'd protect Cady. And put a lie to everything he believed.

If he investigated, he'd find the truth and chance hurting the woman he loved.

Either way, he lost.

He rarely sat behind his desk this long and never to question his own ethics. Right and wrong had always been clear to him. He'd never crossed the line between right and wrong, had never been tempted.

Now he was. Because of a woman.

The thought ground into him like a dull knife peeling away strips of flesh. He discovered that his mouth was parched, his throat dry. He took the few steps to the barrel of water, slid the dipper in, took a sip. It eased the dryness but not the pain.

Cady made the trip to the homestead without conscious thought. When she arrived, she looked about, surprised that she had no memory of the trip home.

But, once inside, she didn't go to Sam's room.

What was she afraid of? The answer slammed into her with the force of a tornado. That Jeb Lassiter's accusations were true? That Sam had betrayed the very people he'd sworn to protect? That the man she'd looked up to, had loved all her life, had fallen?

No!

Even forming the words silently in her mind had her trembling. How could she, for even a minute, believe that Sam might be guilty? Jeb's words ambushed her, and for a moment she felt as though she'd plunged into one of the icy mountain streams of the Colorado Rockies.

The air wheezed in her lungs, then caught, until she was gulping for another breath. She ordered herself to breathe, slow and steady.

The quiet of the cabin mocked the voices screaming in her head, each demanding attention, each giving no quarter. When she could stand it no longer, she pressed her hands to her ears, trying to block them out.

The voices won.

"All right," she said. "I'll prove you're wrong, Jeb Lassiter." *And you, Ford McKinnon.*

Cady realized she'd been holding her breath. Air returned to her lungs in a great rush.

Look for the truth, wherever it lies. In the end, it's the only thing that matters.

Sam's words echoed in the raging silence of Cady's mind. They didn't calm her, but they did make it possible to move forward.

She would find the truth, and, when she did, she'd prove to Ford that he was wrong.

Cady's resentment simmered all over again.

If he thought she would go quietly home and do nothing, he didn't know her. Maybe that was the problem. They really didn't know each other.

Sam's room had always been off-limits. "A man's

got to have a place where he can be private-like," he'd said.

She'd understood. He'd been on duty most every day for twenty-five years, and every man, woman, and child felt free to call upon him for anything.

She hadn't entered his room since going through Sam's papers shortly after his death.

Stomach churning, she took a breath and pushed open the door. Musty air enveloped her. The room was a masculine refuge of log walls and animal heads. She pictured Sam in the battered chair, hands behind his head, feet propped up on the desk.

She straightened her shoulders and headed to it. Scarred with burns and gouges, the desk was a map of Sam's life. She traced a particularly deep scratch, remembering how he'd refused to remove his spurs before planting his boots on the desk he'd built with his own hands.

Happier memories faded as she pulled open the first drawer. The confusion that greeted her had her eyes filling with tears as memories filled her heart. Sam had always been a pack rat, saving everything. Papers, books, and files were jumbled together.

Systematically, she worked her way through the drawers, just as she had before. Her breath came easier now. Nothing she'd found so far was the least bit incriminating.

Jeb Lassiter had lied, obviously trying to get back at Sam. Well, it wasn't going to work.

The next drawer yielded folders of newspaper clippings chronicling rustling in other towns. Well, nothing unusual there.

She started to close the drawer, but it jammed against something. When her attempts to free it failed, she pulled the drawer out completely. Taped to the bottom was another folder.

A glance through its contents revealed bills. Overdue, by the look of them. The words SECOND NOTICE were stamped across many. Some sported a third warning. Her fingers were shaking by the time she finished sorting through them.

How had things gotten so bad? The ranch had never been a moneymaker, not like the surrounding ones whose owners worked them full-time. But it had never lost money.

Her frown deepened as she realized she didn't know how the ranch had fared during the last few years when she'd been away at school. Her attempts to ask Sam about it had always met with an easy assurance that things were fine.

Maybe she hadn't wanted to know. The knowledge caused a well of shame to form inside her. A second set of bills, each bearing a later date than those in the first pile, bore a PAID stamp across them.

Fear dragged at her, fear that Jeb wasn't lying. Fear that maybe she hadn't known Sam at all. Her palms damp, her heart racing, she fought to hold on to a scrap of hope.

So, Sam had come into some money. Maybe a long-lost relative had died, leaving him a substantial inheritance. Maybe he'd taken on some extra work.

"All right," she murmured to herself. "Sam had a few extra dollars. That doesn't mean he's guilty."

Though the words were scarcely a whisper, she wished they didn't sound so hollow. She still wanted, desperately wanted, to believe them, but the stash of paid bills threatened her faith and chipped away the righteous indignation that had sustained her.

Without that, she had little to cling to, except her love for a man who had served his town and its people unselfishly for over half his life.

It was enough, she told herself fiercely.

She scraped her hands down her skirt and forced herself to continue. Her search produced one more piece of the puzzle—a letter from a bank in a neighboring town.

The fact that Sam had any correspondence with a bank outside of Colorado Springs was odd enough. He had banked at Colorado Springs' bank from before she was born. Her fingers icy, she opened the letter. It contained only two items. A bankbook and a deed to the ranch with the notice PAID IN FULL.

How had he managed it? As far as she knew, the ranch still carried a mortgage. She set the deed aside and opened the book.

What she saw there caused her breath to catch. For

each of the eighteen months before Sam's death, a deposit for three hundred dollars showed. No explanation for the money was given. Six months ago, a substantial withdrawal had been made. Though she knew the answer, she made herself scan the mortgage once more. The date there coincided with the withdrawal date listed.

Her fingers curled around the slim book. It didn't mean anything, she told herself. The money could have come from anywhere.

Over two thousand dollars? her mind scoffed. For all the years she was growing up, Sam hadn't had twenty dollars in savings, much less two thousand.

Tucked inside the book was a much-creased paper. Carefully, she pulled it out and smoothed the wrinkles from it. A lump lodged in her throat as she recognized Sam's writing. Cramped and obviously labored, it spoke of his pain more eloquently than any words. It had her eyes stinging with tears as she tried to focus. A hollow opened up in the pit of her stomach as she read.

Cady-did,
If you've found this, it means I'm gone. I've got nothing to leave you but the ranch. I wanted more for you. It's not much, but it's your legacy. Think of your old man, and know that he loves you. Forgive me.
Sam

Forgive me. Two small words that said it all.

She'd been right. Sam hadn't been greedy, at least not for himself. But for her.

She checked the date. Only two days before he had died. She gripped a handful of her shirtwaist over her heart, as if that could hold it together. It seemed to be collapsing inside her chest.

The letter fell from lifeless fingers. For the first time in her life, she feared she might faint. Darkness teased the corners of her eyes.

She willed away the weakness and stumbled to the outhouse, where she was hideously sick. When her stomach—and her heart—were empty, she stumbled out again. She made it as far as the scrap of a kitchen. She slumped to the wood floor and lay there in a heap.

She rose on bones that seemed suddenly old and tired. It took more effort than she believed possible to sit, then stand. She took her time. It was a test of strength, determination.

She pieced together the image of Sam's face in her mind, then closed her eyes.

That, too, was a kind of test.

With the picture of Sam etched in her mind, she let the memories flow.

When she was a child, Sam had let her follow him around and help him clean the sheriff's office. He'd bought her a secondhand saddle and taught her to ride. He'd always had time to teach her the things she couldn't learn in books.

A man like that couldn't—wouldn't—betray his friends. He couldn't be a loving father and a rustler. Could he? Wouldn't she have sensed that Sam was capable of such a thing? Wouldn't she have *known*?

Which could she accept? Her own guilt or Sam's? Both left her with gut-knotting pain.

Sam had been a bigger-than-life figure in Colorado Springs for more than twenty-five years, but to her he had been simply her father, who had seen everything that was good inside her and taught her to see the same.

He had not only taught her the difference between right and wrong but had lived it as well. She'd patterned herself after him. And what did that say about her?

Claws of doubt latched on to the burden she already carried. Pain twisted around her heart like barbs. She drew a deep breath, then shuddered it out. Beneath the tearing grief was anger. She wasn't sure whether it was directed at Sam or herself. She had put him on a pedestal, and, when he'd fallen, as idols were apt to do, she'd blamed him.

She roused herself enough to make a small fire in the hearth. She stirred the embers and watched the flames flicker to life, praying some of the heat they generated would penetrate her icy skin.

Despite the warmth, the cold inside her deepened.

She curled up in Sam's favorite chair, as if its arms could comfort her as his had. She wrapped her own arms around herself and began to rock. The motion soothed her ragged nerves, but it didn't block out the pain.

For that she found no comfort at all.

Chapter Nine

With the morning sun still only a promise, Cady made her way to the town cemetery. She'd spent a fitful night, her mind whirling in painful circles.

The Colorado Springs Cemetery was a small one. It had started as a family plot. Over the years, it had been added to in piecemeal fashion until it resembled a faded patchwork quilt. Atop a hill, it captured the wind.

It was the loneliest sight she'd ever seen.

Picking her way over the uneven ground to Sam's grave, Cady clasped her arms around herself against the wind that cut straight to the heart.

She wasn't the only one taking a beating. Trees, their naked branches clacking together like the rhythm sticks the town band used, swayed and bent beneath the wind's savagery. It pared needles from the pines and whipped them about. One struck her cheek with the sting of a whip.

She stared down at the dates engraved into the rough tombstone that told so little about her father. She traced the words carved below the dates. BELOVED FATHER. No mention of his twenty-five years as sheriff.

"Sam!" she cried. "Why?"

Why did you do it? Why didn't you realize that I didn't need, didn't want, anything else besides you?

The howl of the wind was her only answer. She let the tears have their way. The wind picked up, pricking her face with sand, the angry buzz of it reminding her of a nest of rattlers. Still, she didn't move and mourned the man her father had been, the man he had become. How could she reconcile the two?

She didn't try deceiving herself into believing that these were the only tears she would shed. She wasn't ashamed of them. Tears were nature's way of washing away pain.

Still, her emotions felt scraped raw.

The peace she'd hoped to find was absent. If she'd come home more, if she'd been more available, if she'd insisted Sam share his problems, maybe he wouldn't have felt compelled to steal from his neighbors, his friends.

She recognized the doubts for what they were,

heavy-duty guilt that was as insidious as it was incessant. It hammered at her, mocking all that she believed about Sam, about herself.

For her, Sam had died yesterday—when she found the letter.

Her mind spun, images of Sam and herself all racing through her brain, reeling even faster, confusing her, taunting her with memories now turned bittersweet.

She was four, and Sam was setting her on her first pony, a small paint. . . . She was nine and finding the dictionary he'd sent away to Denver for to surprise her for her birthday. . . . She was thirteen, and he presented her with Cheyenne, a beautiful gelding with a heart as big as the Colorado sky. . . . She was twenty, and Sam held her as she gulped back sobs when Cheyenne broke his leg in a gopher hole and had to be put down.

Simple things, but Sam Armstrong had been a simple man. He'd never sought attention for doing his job, never even asked for thanks. He'd done the job and done it well.

For as long as she could remember, Sam had been the ideal by which she'd measured every other man. He'd been her hero, her best friend, and everything else. Perhaps that was why she could never feel anything more than friendship for the boys who'd squired her to the town dances and picnics. None had come up to scratch.

Until Ford.

Sam had brought her up to believe that true richness had nothing to do with the size of your bank account and everything to do with the strength of your character. What had turned him from a man who had never cheated anyone in his life to someone who stole from his neighbors?

Darkness closed around her as questions spiraled through her mind. Deliberately, she concentrated on the sun climbing in the eastern sky. The sky brightened with every minute she stood there. It helped ease the chill around her heart.

The scream was ripped from her. But it wasn't Sam's name that she called. It was Ford's.

What was wrong with her? She wasn't some soft city girl looking for a man to come to her rescue. She was a strong, capable woman, one who had been looking out for herself for years now.

Yet all she could think of was Ford. She needed him, needed his strength when her own was lacking, needed his laughter to replace what she could no longer summon.

The admission gave her pause. When had she come to the point of needing a man—a certain man—more than she needed her next breath?

She looked up, mildly surprised to see that the sun still shone. A chill spread down her arms, one that had nothing to do with the sharp bite of the cold.

The wind complained again, its lament a soulful counterpoint to her own tormented thoughts.

Why?

She had no answers. At least no answers she was ready to face. Sam had made his choices. He'd lived with them. She had no doubt that the guilt had eaten at him, perhaps even bringing on the heart attack.

Sam had lived his life by a rigid code of honor. How could he have tossed it away? She couldn't make sense of what he'd done any more than she could her own feelings about it.

Ford gazed at the solitary figure. Framed by the gray light of morning, she stood, head bowed, hands outstretched as though reaching for something.

Compassion stirred inside him at the lonely sight she made.

He'd questioned Jeb, going over dates and places. The details the rustler gave came too rapidly, too easily to dismiss. And sometime during the night, Ford admitted to himself that he believed the man. Sam Armstrong *had* turned a blind eye to the rustling.

When Ford hadn't found Cady at the homestead, he'd made the short trip to the cemetery. His hunch had been right.

At the cemetery's entrance, Ford dismounted with a murmured order for Hawk to stay. For long minutes, he waited, wanting to give her the privacy she needed. He leaned into the teeth of the wind, bracing himself against its force.

Cries—not hot, passionate ones but slow, aching ones—echoed over the prairie. Ones that bled out of the soul.

He couldn't bear it a moment longer and started toward her. He could have sworn he actually felt her pain, felt it shiver over him. He ached to hold her, to tell her everything would be all right. He would have taken her pain twice over, more, if it would only spare her.

She looked up at his approach. Her eyes widened, only the silvery sheen on her cheeks betraying recently shed tears.

He knew you had to face the first grief alone before you could accept comfort. And maybe she wouldn't or couldn't accept comfort from him no matter how long he waited. Something twisted inside him with painful intensity.

Ford noted that she had wiped her expression clean. Pretty neat trick, he thought. Too bad it wasn't going to work. He looked more closely and saw her eyes so tight, they hurt him, her posture taut as pain.

He closed the small distance between them, needing to hold her, to reassure her that this hadn't changed anything between them.

Pain shuddered from her, great, palpable waves of it. He longed to cut through it, to strip it away from the woman he loved.

"Cady." Only that. Her name. It was all he could think to say.

The sheen of new tears had him closing his arms around her. He pressed her against his chest and held her. For a moment, she leaned against him, leaned on him.

Then she pulled back. He knew her independence wouldn't allow her to lean on him, on anyone, for very long.

Confusion clouded her eyes for a fraction of a second. Determination took its place. Once more he was reminded that this woman had both guts and courage.

She looked small and lost and fragile, not nearly strong enough to fight off all the feelings that Sam's betrayal must have stirred up.

The shadows in her eyes reached inside him, and he felt as if there were iron bands squeezing around his heart.

He watched as she squared her shoulders, giving an impression of size even though she was barely bigger than a minute. She was a survivor, strong in herself, which still allowed her infinite compassion for others.

The line of her shoulders told him just how tightly she was holding herself together.

He laid a hand on her arm and turned her toward him. The muscles of her arm stiffened under his hand.

"You were right," she said, her voice but a whisper

in the pale light. "Sam was in on the rustling, almost from the beginning."

They'd see this through together.

Ford knew how hard it was for her to say that— and how necessary. The hollowness in her voice was as unmistakable as the lines of pain and heartache etching her features.

Though her face was ashen, it was set with fierce determination. He looked at the strong line of her back and reminded himself that, no matter how fragile she appeared at the moment, she had a reserve of courage and grit.

She blinked several times as though holding back tears. A low, choppy moan rose from her chest. She looked up at him, her eyes luminous and so full of anguish that Ford couldn't help pulling her into his arms.

She resisted at first, but he murmured, "Don't pull away. Even if you don't need to be held, I need to hold you." It must have been the right thing to say, because she finally relaxed against him.

She looked vulnerable. Defenseless. And in desperate need of a friend.

Cady was anything but helpless, he reminded himself, no matter how beaten she seemed right now. She had a right to grieve and to come to her own acceptance of Sam and what he'd done.

Ford had no doubt that she would emerge from her anguish stronger than ever.

He knew she had to work this through on her own. He also knew she needed to work through her feelings her own way. It was only natural to pull her into his arms, to press her tear-streaked face against his shoulder.

She held up a hand. "Don't." Her voice frayed, then steadied. "I went through Sam's papers. Found a bankbook." A beat of silence passed. Another. "It must feel good. Knowing you were right."

He took the verbal blow. What else could he do? It wasn't temper sparking her eyes. That would have been easy to fight. It was weariness. And pain.

He didn't say anything, only pulled her into his arms once more and held on. He slid a hand to her nape and pressed her face to his chest, his other arm sliding around her waist.

He watched her struggle to rein in her emotions. He felt her initial resistance and ignored it. When he made it plain he wasn't letting go, she melted into him.

Rage at Sam Armstrong poured through his veins, but he kept his voice even, his words gentle. "I don't care what Sam did. It's over."

"Is it?"

"If you let it be."

He knew it wasn't that simple. He let the silence stretch, torn between duty and how he'd like to handle the situation if things had been different.

"Why? Why did he do it?"

The agony behind the question brought a hard lump to Ford's throat. He knew Cady wasn't seeking an answer, only giving voice to her bewilderment.

He remembered his own despair at the death of his parents. How much worse was it for Cady, having to accept not only Sam's death but his betrayal of everything he believed in as well?

"I owe you an apology," she said.

Whatever he'd expected her to say, that wasn't it.

"I wanted to blame you. And I did. I wanted you to be wrong. I didn't want to believe that Sam . . . that Sam could be part of it." She swallowed. "I'm sorry."

"It's forgotten."

"Don't you understand? Sam was part of it. He didn't just look the other way. He helped set it up. He helped rob his friends, the people he'd sworn to protect." Despair and shame pulled her deeper and deeper into herself.

He knew she needed to talk about Sam's betrayal, and he listened as she poured out her grief.

"Sam was sick," Ford said at last. "He didn't know what he was doing. The question is, can you love the whole man, not just the part that was good and just?"

"I did. I do." She heard the words, and she wanted to believe she'd spoken the truth. Did she love Sam, flaws and all? It shamed her that she didn't have an immediate answer. "How could he have stolen from his neighbors? His friends?" Her voice ached with the enormity of Sam's deception.

Once again, he knew she didn't expect—or want—an answer.

"You don't have to do this alone."

Cady looked, really looked, at the man who had become the most important person in her life. The tenderness in his voice didn't surprise her. Once, it might have. She knew better now and recognized that gentleness was as much a part of him as was the strength he wore so easily.

Pride had kept her silent. Now need gave her voice. Her tone devoid of emotion, she told him what she'd found in Sam's desk.

As she stood there shaking, her defenses in tatters, unable to find the strength to put up even the flimsiest of barricades, she admitted to herself that she wanted the comfort only Ford could offer.

That same pride finally stiffened her backbone, and she took a step away. She needed to get through this on her own.

Hurt shadowed Ford's eyes. She regretted that. Hurting him was the last thing she wanted to do, but if she let her feelings out, she feared she'd crumble.

Pain squeezed her heart as she forced herself to meet his gaze. It was then that she noticed the bleakness in his eyes, the lines of strain around his mouth. A day's growth of beard added to the appearance of weariness. With a flash of insight, she realized the last twenty-four hours had been no easier for him than they had for her.

He had grieved for her, just as she'd grieved for Sam. The knowledge warmed her, despite her misery.

She moved back to him, her steps taking her where her heart longed to be. His arms opened, and she was in them.

For countless moments they stayed there, locked together. She absorbed his strength, his goodness, and knew that she was not alone. Comfort surrounded her, keeping out much of the pain and anguish, as it always did when Ford was near.

"Better?" he asked.

Better? Warmth and safety against the coldness brought on by Sam's betrayal. She nodded against his chest.

"Grieving's work that has to be done. Sam was sick," Ford said again. "He wasn't thinking clearly."

Would others be so understanding, so forgiving? The thought of Calvin Browne brought a frown to her face. He'd take special delight in rubbing her nose in Sam's weakness.

Pettiness like that she could handle. But what of Sam's friends? How could she face them? How could she ask them to look past one mistake and see, instead, the man who had spent most of his adult life serving the town and the people he loved?

"Give them a chance," Ford said, apparently reading her thoughts. "The folks around here are good people. They won't let you down."

"What am I going to do?" she asked, barely aware she spoke the words aloud.

"What would Sam want you to do?"

The first glimmer of a smile touched her lips. "He'd say, tell the truth and to heck with the consequences."

"It sounds like you already know what you have to do," Ford said in his slow way. "Just remember to listen to your heart as well as your head."

"Can I do both?" she asked, more of herself than of him.

It was then that she gave in to the pain. He folded his arms around her and let her weep. Great, gulping sobs shook her body and left her gulping for air. She wrapped her arms around his waist and hung on. He cradled her against him while she cried for herself, for Sam, for the misplaced pride that had driven him to do what he'd done.

Ford made no attempt to stem the flow of tears but let her cry until she was exhausted.

"Cady." There was a wealth of sympathy in the single word, in the thumb that tenderly stroked the wetness coursing down her cheeks.

"I was gone, off chasing a dream, when Sam needed me."

"Getting an education isn't desertion."

As always, Ford knew how to answer her doubts.

She couldn't resist stroking his hard, stubbled cheek, and she felt the power that he held in check.

Gradually, as her tears dried, she recognized a new sensation growing out of the solid comfort she'd felt while sheltered in his arms. A sensation that had nothing to do with comfort and everything to do with the man who held her. She inhaled deeply of his scent, a blend of leather and fresh air, and felt his heartbeat quicken. Her own picked up its pace to match it.

When he brushed his lips against her hair, she didn't pull away. It would take no effort at all to raise her head and meet his lips with hers. To let him continue to hold her and never let go.

Shocked at the direction her thoughts were taking, she took a step back. She looked up at him, then hiccupped. The spell was broken. The look in his eyes warned her, though, that they hadn't finished what they'd started.

He didn't push. For that, she was grateful. *Soon,* his eyes promised.

Her nod, infinitesimal, acknowledged the unspoken notice.

"Feel better?" he asked, stroking the hair back from her damp cheeks.

"I didn't cry at Sam's funeral. I never really allowed myself to cry for him at all. Until now."

The last two words came out in a catching sob that tugged at him with a force more startling than the raw pain he read on her face.

He looked at her eyes, red and swollen, and trembling lips, at the stubborn chin aimed up, and her squared shoulders. Each was part of the woman, the whole of with whom he'd fallen in love.

"Give yourself the chance to grieve for him. It's the only way you'll be able to get over the pain and remember the good times."

"You're right. I guess I didn't want to admit how much I missed him. I thought if I didn't cry, I could pretend that he wasn't gone." She rubbed the heels of her hands across her eyes. "Stupid, huh?"

"Not stupid. Just human." He caught her chin on the ridge of his knuckles. "You know what he believed, what he was. No one can take that from you." He paused. "Unless you let them."

He almost smiled when she lifted her chin. The lady was a fighter. She'd make it through this. *They'd* make it through this. Together.

She wouldn't make it easy, for herself or for him. His lips curved into a rueful smile. He'd always liked a challenge.

He teetered off the narrow ledge he'd been walking and fell headfirst into love with her.

Her beautiful eyes, shiny with just-shed tears, gazed at him gratefully. She was hurting, and he ached to wipe the pain away. But equally strong was the desire to kiss away the last traces of tears, to kiss her slightly parted lips, to kiss *her.*

Every instinct urged Ford to touch her, to draw her

into the circle of his arms, to hold her and never let her go. When the longing grew too great, he jammed his fists into his pockets. When the sweet smell of her hair drifted up to meet him, he turned his head and gently kissed her.

He wanted to tell her he loved her, wanted to ask her to marry him. It didn't seemed fair, though, when she'd been through so much already.

He preferred to play—and fight—fair.

He could wait until the time was right, until the emotional storm she was riding had passed. He knew that only time and grieving would ease the ache in her heart.

He wished he could be sure of her, of what she wanted. One thing he'd learned, though—that with Cady, nothing was sure.

Ford could no longer help himself and touched his lips to hers again. Though he offered the kiss in compassion and understanding, the taste of her lips reminded him of how much more he felt.

He wanted to protect her, to cherish her. . . . He smiled faintly at the word, yet it described his feelings for her. Cady was a woman to be cherished, treasured.

For a long moment he studied her, his gaze moving over her face like a restless wind. It invited her to share her feelings, to tell him everything.

"I feel as if I've lost him all over again. Everything I believed about him, felt for him, was a lie." The words trembled from her lips and cut into her heart like the buck knife Sam had worn tucked inside his boot.

"Don't." Ford brushed his lips against her temples. "Would Sam want you blaming yourself?"

"No." The answer came swiftly and without hesitation.

"You loved your pa. That was no lie. He loved you. That was no lie either."

"I wanted to blame you." She could make the admission now.

"I know." Ford waited.

"I'm not going to punish you for something you had nothing to do with."

She splayed her hands into his dark hair. It curled around her fingers. She rested her head against his shoulder. It felt solid, strong, like the rest of him.

"I'm going to have to ask you some questions, see the letter you found."

She nodded.

They walked back to the cabin. Numbly, she showed him the letter.

It made it easier, Ford being the one to ask her the questions. And it made it harder.

"When you're ready to talk, I'll be here," he said when he had finished questioning her. "I wish I could fix it for you. Make everything all right." The tug in his voice told her that this was almost as hard on him as it was on her.

"I'm old enough to fix things for myself. I'd rather have a friend than a rescuer."

"I can be both."

"I'm counting on it."

Chapter Ten

Cady locked the door to the *Gazette,* something she'd never done before. A newspaper, she'd always thought, should welcome the people whose lives it chronicled.

Work, the balm that had seen her through her grief at Sam's death, now became duty, a duty to the people of Colorado Springs. To Sam. To herself.

She was a journalist. Her integrity demanded that she write the truth, just as Ford had had to discover the truth about the rustling. The analogy put things into perspective.

Cady Armstrong stood by her principles, faced her responsibilities. Sam had taught her that, to own up to whatever she'd done. He'd expect the same of her now. Especially now.

His voice, as strong as though he were standing next to her, echoed through her mind. *You best swallow it down, Cady-did, 'cause that's the way it's gonna stick.* A smile curled around her heart at the name only Sam had called her. *Cady-did.*

She wrote the story of Sam's involvement in the rustling, neither overdramatizing it nor underplaying it. They were the hardest words she'd ever written.

He did it for me.

The knowledge was a dull pain in her chest, and that pain was a dark thing that drove her.

It was, of course, front-page news. It would be treated as such. There wouldn't be an editorial, though. She didn't have the heart for it.

She didn't pretend to herself that the news wouldn't spread through the town like a prairie fire. It would reach every corner, from the ladies' quilting circle to the meeting of the church elders to the men who gathered at the saloon. By tomorrow, everyone in Colorado Springs would know that Sam Armstrong had betrayed them.

She didn't care for herself. As far as she was concerned, people could flap their jaws as much as they wanted. But she cared deeply that anyone would utter a harsh word against the man she had loved with every beat of her heart.

She liked to believe that the choices of his last years were not indicative of the person he had been. Sam was dead, beyond the reach of her anger or pity or sad dreams of how things might have been different if she'd been around more.

She worked steadily, methodically setting print. Gradually, the repetitive task began to soothe her. The rhythm of muscles working together and the trickle of sweat between her shoulder blades comforted her as she cranked the press.

The first copy appeared. She scanned the story, then nodded her approval. It was, she thought with irony, her best writing to date.

When Emilie knocked at the door, Cady didn't turn her away but welcomed her friend inside. She'd avoided Emilie up until now, preferring to handle her pain herself. Her mouth took on the brittle edges of a false smile.

The frank sympathy in Emilie's eyes convinced Cady she'd been wrong to keep her heartache to herself.

"I'm sorry." The simple words said everything that needed saying.

Somehow Cady found herself in Emilie's arms, and, to Cady's surprise, she felt like talking.

Emilie listened as Cady tried to make sense of what she was feeling.

"I wasn't here for him when he needed me. That's why he did what he did." Once again, guilt carved her heart into tiny pieces.

Emilie gazed at Cady with profound gentleness, obviously aching to reach out. But Cady's loss was untouchable, and her friend understood that. "Sam wouldn't want you blaming yourself," Emilie said with conviction.

"He was your pa," she added. "He loved you. In the end, that's all that matters."

"Ford said the same thing," Cady murmured, more to herself than to her friend.

"He's a good man."

Cady summoned a smile. "You don't have to convince me of that." She handed a paper to Emilie. "Read it, and tell me what you think."

While Cady waited, Emilie read, then looked up. "You didn't have to do this."

"That's where you're wrong."

"You are the strongest woman I know," Emilie said, and she reached for Cady's hand, tears gathering in her eyes.

Cady squeezed her friend's hand. "Thank you. And speaking of strong, you're pretty great in that area yourself."

Emilie wiped her eyes. "I never would have had the courage to leave Cal if not for you."

Cady did some eye-wiping of her own. "You would have. You're too smart to have stayed with him."

"You're right."

Cady heard the smallest lift of pride in Emilie's voice and found she could smile after all. "Now, before this mutual admiration society gets out of hand, let's get this paper delivered."

They spent the next hours distributing the paper. Copies were snatched up with ill-concealed enthusiasm. The news, Cady thought, had already made the rounds. The people only wanted to see what she had done with it. All were clearly torn between an avid desire to question her about Sam's part in the rustling and an identical desire to offer support.

In the end, curiosity and sympathy were dispensed in equal doses. She accepted each, philosophical about the one and grateful for the other.

Ford read the article, then read it again. The words had a starkness to them that belied the emotion he knew was behind the report.

He doubled the paper, stuck it into his back pocket, and headed to the *Gazette*. He wasn't surprised that Cady had written the article, nor that she hadn't tried to whitewash Sam's guilt. The straightforward story said as much about her as it did about Sam.

When, Ford wondered, had he gotten to the point where he needed to see Cady, if only for a moment, to make his day complete?

He found her bent over a desk, brow furrowed in concentration as she wrote. He cupped her elbows, lifted her to her feet, and turned her toward him.

She nestled her head on his chest. The tenderness of the gesture moved him unbearably.

The guilt and grief on her face were so naked that he felt as though he were intruding on a private moment.

He stroked her hair. "We'll see this through. To-gether."

If he could, he'd spare her the pain of having Sam's part in the rustling made public. He knew the news would spread.

He also knew she was still reeling from shock. With time, she'd come to terms with it. She was a strong woman. He was only beginning to learn just how strong.

What they felt for each other had evolved into something more, though, something that went far beyond simple friendship. *Love.* The word wouldn't be denied any longer.

It scared him, the intensity of his feelings. He'd never used the word *love* preceded by *I* and followed by *you.* Not even with Margaret. He'd thought he loved her, but something had held him back from uttering the words.

This needing to be with Cady every moment, to share the good times and the bad—was that really love? Or was it simply a temporary attraction that would fade with the passage of time?

Without stopping to think about it, he bent to brush a kiss against her lips.

He was drawn to her in a way that defied logic. He searched his thoughts and emotions about Cady.

"I've been taking care of myself a long time, so I'm not in the market for a nursemaid."

"If you were half as smart as you pretend to be, you'd know why I'm here."

She shivered at the anger in his tone, anger she knew she'd sown with her own pride. She placed a hand on his arm. "I'm sorry."

He shook it off. "Are you?" His tone softened fractionally. "Pride's all well and good. But it won't give comfort."

His words settled over her with unmistakable truth. She flinched at the bald facts he'd served her, the unapologetic boldness of them.

She almost gave in to the need to lean against him again. She could lay her head on his shoulder, close her eyes, and pretend everything was all right.

"Don't shut me out," he said, the words quietly spoken but insistent nonetheless.

"I don't want to," she murmured.

"Then let me help you."

"It's not your problem," she said stiffly.

"If it hurts you, it is."

The long look he gave her missed nothing. Her face was whiter than a trout's belly, but the quiet confidence in her voice told him she had spoken the truth. She was all right. She was a lot more than that, his heart whispered. He couldn't fault her for having a wagonload of pride, even if it were misplaced. It was, he knew, a chore to swallow pride.

He urged her down and sat beside her. Gently but

insistently, he raised her chin so that she was forced to look at him. "There's something special between us," he told her quietly. "If you're honest, you won't deny it." He waited for her answer.

Her nod was barely there, but it was enough. "Almost from the start."

Her honesty, as bright as the Colorado sun, touched him as nothing else could.

She reached up to kiss him.

Tenderness, sweet as the lips he'd so recently kissed, curled inside him. He loved this woman. She was all that he wanted. But there was no way to overcome the fact that he would always be linked in her mind with the unraveling of Sam's part in the rustling. Was that too big a hurdle for them to cross?

Whatever their differences, they'd find a way to resolve them. They had to. The stakes were too great for it to be otherwise.

Soft color spilled into her cheeks, but she didn't turn away. Her gaze remained locked with his, her eyes silently telling him what he longed to hear.

"I don't think—"

"Don't think. Just feel." He kissed her again.

"You're good to me," she said. "Good *for* me."

"I know." And, he thought, it was time she figured that out.

She laughed. The sound surprised her. She couldn't remember the last time she'd let loose a real belly laugh. Slowly, she shook her head. She *could* remember. She'd laughed with all the abandon of a child when she and Ford had taken a picnic into the mountains—before Lassiter's accusations had turned her world upside down.

That world had tilted, but she was regaining her balance.

"I want to hate him, but I still love him," Cady said in a low voice.

"Sure you do. He was your pa. He loved you. He might have lost his way for a bit, but that doesn't change what he felt for you. What you felt for him."

"Thank you," Cady whispered.

"My pa used to say that love and hate are horns on the same bull's head."

She held on to that over the next few weeks, held on with both hands.

Friends rallied around her. Enemies seemd to crawl out of the woodwork to toss taunts and jecrs her way. She refused to hide, refused to bow her head in the face of their censure.

Throughout it all, Ford was there for her, his quiet support more precious than a pot of gold nuggets.

That gave her pause. Ford had quickly become the most important person in her life. She hadn't planned for it to happen, but it had.

Sam hadn't been perfect. He had been human, flawed and imperfect. She could accept that. More, she could live with it.

Some folks saw fit to shoot spiteful arrows in her direction. They were nothing, though, compared to the layers of sticky guilt she heaped upon herself.

It was ironic that Sam's own words kept her going. She remembered asking him how he'd managed when her mother took off when she, Cady, had been little more than a baby.

His eyes had taken on a faraway look, and she knew he was remembering. *Don't look too far ahead. Take it one day at a time. That's all you can do.*

She had cause to recall the words many times over the next weeks.

Just when she believed the worst was over, Cal Browne sauntered into the office.

"Heard about your pa. A common thief. Aren't so high-and-mighty anymore, are you?" Thin lips drew flat over yellowed teeth. Mean eyes grew dark with victory. Savage satisfaction shaded his voice. His words were deliberately cruel, but Cady refused to let the hurt take hold.

"What's the matter, girlie? No highfalutin words about right and wrong?" The words snapped out like savage fangs while triumph tightened his heavy jowls.

Despite her determination to ignore the man's mocking comments, grief ambushed her. She took a moment to smooth away the ripples of pain. "Sam made a mistake. That doesn't mean I have to sit around and listen to a snake like you spew your venom. Now, get out."

"Folks around here don't like cattle thieves. Or the daughter of one." Lines of hatred gouged the skin around his eyes.

The jibe found its target and stuck. She flinched at the triumph in Browne's eyes, then steeled herself and her pride. At the same time, she dug deep for some of the grit Sam had instilled within her.

"That's the only way someone like you can feel good about himself—taking potshots at a dead man." She let the contempt ooze through her words.

Some of the pleasure in his expression faded. He wasn't done with her yet, though. "Looks like you won't be sticking your nose into other people's business much longer." With that, he took himself off.

The door slammed, only to be opened within a few seconds. Thinking Browne had returned, she looked up, ready to do battle.

Emilie walked in. She took a look at Cady's stricken face and grimaced. "I saw Cal hightailing it out of here. He was in such an all-fired hurry that he didn't even see me." She drew a shaky breath. "Has he been spreading his poison about Sam?"

Cady's silence was answer enough.

"He's not worth worrying about. I should know," Emilie said with heavy irony. "The people around here aren't going to let one mistake wipe out all the good Sam did for this town."

Cady dredged up a smile. "I appreciate that. But not everyone feels that way." Even she could hear the dejection in her voice. She no longer tried to pretend she didn't care.

"Don't sell 'em short," Emilie said.

Cady's smile came more easily this time.

She worked through the afternoon. For once, Cady's mind wasn't on the past, but the present . . . and the future.

Something special, Ford had said. Did he mean love?

Love for her was a total commitment that put the other person before everything and everyone else. It was caring for him more than you cared about yourself. It was wanting his happiness, even at the expense of your own. It was finding joy in simply being with him and knowing that joy again in memory.

Relief poured through her that they had been able to confront the pain of Sam's deceit and come away from it stronger than ever. Ford had stayed by her side throughout the aftermath. She would forever be grateful for his support and belief in her.

She thought of her own feelings. What she felt for Ford wasn't something she'd been able to look at too closely. For one thing, Sam was still very much in her mind, and until her feelings about what he'd done were resolved, it wouldn't be fair to Ford to offer him less than her whole self. It wouldn't be fair to her either, because too many of her feelings were tied up in the past.

She'd taken to spending evenings outside. Twilight had thickened, the hazy clouds of late afternoon chased away by the deeper shades of evening. Amethyst shadows dimpled the ground, their shapes ever shifting, phantoms of the growing darkness.

She lifted her head, wanting to catch a bit of breeze. The cool air caressed her skin.

The shock of learning about Sam had still not completely receded, but she was beginning to come to terms with it. It had rocked her picture of him . . . and of herself. She'd had to face up to some unpalatable truths.

The soul-searching had not been pleasant, and she had shrunk from the opening up of old wounds. Understanding the need that had driven Sam to do what he did, she could forgive him. It seemed that most of the town had decided to remember the man and not the mistake.

She knew she had Ford to thank for much of that. Quietly, subtly, he'd let the town know of his own feelings about Sam. She had Ford to thank for a lot of things.

The following day, she talked with Horace Silas, the president of the bank, and arranged to put up the house and acreage for sale.

"I can't promise much," Silas said with an apologetic shrug. "But we'll get enough to pay back . . ." His voice trailed off, and a dull flush colored his face.

Recognizing that his embarrassment was for her, Cady nodded. "Thank you."

"I don't mind telling you that the money will come in mighty handy to the folks around here."

"I'd appreciate it if you could see to it that the money is distributed fairly."

"I'll see to it personally."

When the telegram arrived, Ford opened it, read it, then read it again. The job of United States marshal was his.

Did he want to accept?

Did he? Of course he did. It was what he'd worked toward for the last ten years.

What of Cady? Would she come with him?

His heart gave a fierce kick as he thought of her. She was a complex mixture of vulnerability and strength, uncertainty and valor. He liked her grit, her boldness, her integrity.

As long as he lived, he would never forget her courage, the kind it took for a daughter to report her father's betrayal of his friends and neighbors.

Cady Armstrong had more brains and courage than most men he knew. She gave as good as she got and then some. She was his equal in every sense of the word. In addition, she had an air of quiet restfulness that let him sink into his own thoughts when he needed to.

She was also as obstinate as two mules pulling in opposite directions and twice as feisty. Maybe that was why he loved her as he did. A grin tempted the corners of his mouth as he remembered their first meeting.

She was brave and valiant, with a determination that continued to amaze him. She had guts. She'd proved that when she'd stood up to Calvin Browne. More, she had humanity. She'd shown that when she'd taken Emilie Browne into her home and her heart.

In all his years of searching, Ford had never found a moment when he could say, "Life doesn't get any better than this." That day, he found it.

He made a trip to the General Mercantile. Jensen didn't carry much in the way of jewelry, but he did have gold bands. Ford made his selection, smiling as he thought of how the ring would look on Cady's hand.

The gold band fit snugly inside the back pocket of his trousers. It belonged on her finger.

Chapter Eleven

Ford had taken to stopping by as she closed down the *Gazette* for the evening. It was a habit, Cady thought, that she could quickly become accustomed to.

Tonight was no different. Her heartbeat tripped over itself in her pleasure at seeing him.

Her smile bloomed at the warmth she read in his eyes.

"Doris' meat loaf is the special of the day at the cafe," he said. "If you haven't eaten, I'd appreciate company for dinner."

"Doris's meat loaf is a treat not to be missed." She wiped the ink from her hands and attempted to straighten her hair.

"Let me," Ford said, and he tucked a stray strand behind her ear. He waited while she locked the door to the *Gazette,* then, with a hand cupping her elbow, walked with her to the cafe.

The meat loaf was as good as promised, the faint breeze pleasantly cool.

Under Ford's gentle questioning, she found herself telling him more about Sam.

"He could dance me into the ground," she said, her voice so low, it barely registered over the buzz of others. "He'd wipe the sweat off his face and start all over again, laughing so hard, he could barely stand. He loved apple cake and was forever asking me to make one for him." A sob caught in her throat. "I wish I could make him just one more."

Gradually, she grew aware that Ford wasn't only asking questions but reminding her of all that she loved about Sam. As she talked, she realized that the memories no longer made her sad but lifted her heart as not much else ever had.

"Thank you."

"For what?"

"Giving the best of Sam back to me." Thanks to Ford, she could hold those memories in her heart without the pain of the last weeks.

Then she remembered. She had to tell him what she'd planned.

"I'm putting the ranch up for sale." The catch in her voice betrayed her. She had fought with herself over the decision, then had done what she'd known she had to.

"Why?"

"I can't keep it."

"Because of what Sam did?"

Her nod felt as shaky as her voice. "He paid off the note on the ranch with money from the rustling." She'd already figured she could pay back what Sam had taken if she sold everything.

"We can't prove Sam used his share of the rustling money to pay off the ranch."

"I don't care about proof. I know what he did. What I have to do." There was that hitch in her voice again, mortifying her. "I can't keep it. Not when I know . . ." She didn't continue. The grief was still too fresh, too new.

The approval in his eyes told her he'd have done the same thing in her place. The knowledge warmed her, even as her heart was close to breaking. The homestead had been in her family for more than eighty years.

She would be the one to sell it. She felt as if she was betraying generations of Armstrongs. The guilt of selling the land placed in her trust yawned at the back of her mind like a bottomless pit waiting for her to trip. She didn't expect top dollar, not with the run-down condition of the place.

"I've got some money put by if—"

"I don't take charity." Even the word stung.

His eyes were no longer warm. "*Charity* isn't a word that belongs between friends."

She spread her hands in a contrite gesture. "I'm sorry."

"Let me help you. We could make it a loan—"

"I can't. I have to take care of this on my own."

"That's pride talking."

Not just pride. It was Sam. He had instilled the fierce pride in her she couldn't shake, even if she wanted to. With a flash of insight, she realized that anger lay beneath her pride. Suddenly, she was tired of both the anger and the pride. "I can't take your money. But thank you. You don't know what it means to me."

She'd hurt Ford with her refusal. She knew it but was powerless to change what she was. Who she was. She'd manage. Somehow. She'd spent most of her life hardscrabble poor. It wasn't such a hardship being without. She'd done some ciphering and figured she could hold on to the paper—barely.

She'd make it. Sam had claimed that Armstrongs had a stubborn streak in them. Right now, she'd need that and more to make things right for the townspeople and for herself.

The crushing guilt that had choked her upon learning of Sam's part in the rustling had eased. The growing hope that she and Ford were about to reach a new and maybe permanent step in their relationship lifted the burden even more. She looked to the future with an eagerness that surprised and delighted her.

"The editor of the Denver paper has been following

my series of articles about the rustling. He was impressed." He was more than that, she thought with a rush of pride. The telegram she'd received had been expansive in its praise. She'd be writing a daily editorial, reporting as well. "He wants me to do a regular column for the paper. The best part is, I can stay right here. In the Springs."

"Wouldn't it be easier to move to Denver?"

She shook her head. "I can send the stories by telegraph. He already has reporters in Denver. He wants a different perspective."

"That's great." The words were right, but the tone wasn't.

The day had darkened. Had the remaining bit of sun slipped behind a cloud? Suddenly the thrill of reaching a lifelong goal didn't have quite the shine it should have.

"Is something wrong?"

"I've been offered the job of United States marshal. I'll be leaving for Denver at the end of the month."

Denver. Not so far away that they couldn't see each other occasionally, but too far away to make a life together.

She gulped down her disappointment. "That's wonderful." She thought of what that meant and knew that Ford's dream was every bit as important to him as hers was to her.

"I want you to come with me."

She groped for words. Hadn't she just been dreaming of a future with him? The dream did an abrupt about-face.

He skimmed his knuckles across her cheek. "I know how much the paper means to you."

Her heart stumbled. She could easily trip, fall. Her feelings for him were tangling her into knots. How could he suggest she give up everything she'd worked so hard for? Didn't he understand that her whole life had been leading up to this one point?

Pain squeezed her heart as she looked at him. "Do you? Do you know that I worked eight years for this chance? Do you know that while other girls were going to dances, I was home studying? Learning how to write, how to operate a press?"

"You can have both."

At last she put into words what had hung between them since he made his announcement.

"I belong here, Ford. The Springs is my home. My family."

That wasn't all of it. She thought of her mother's desertion. She knew it had affected her, prodding her fear of loving too deeply, as Sam had. She also knew it had crippled the few courtships she'd allowed herself. She'd never permitted herself to commit fully to any of the men she'd allowed to court her.

Years ago, she'd found the one picture Sam had kept of her mother. A pretty enough woman, though there was a remote look in her eyes.

Cady had never put words to her fears. Until now. What was there about Ford that made her tell him things she'd never confided to anyone else? Even Sam.

She had her answer in the understanding she saw in his eyes the moment she spoke of her mother.

"You may look like her, but you're not like her," he said at the end of her recitation. "What you start, you finish."

Did she? she wondered. "I left Sam. Just when he needed me."

"Seems to me he's the one who pushed you to leave. He knew you were pining to go to Boston. He wanted that for you."

"And he stole to pay for it." She couldn't keep the heartache from her voice.

"Sam's choices were his own. No one's blaming you. Not for any of it."

She wished she didn't blame herself.

"You're not your ma. Or your pa. He did what he thought he had to. Just like you will. The only question is whether you're going to let the past decide what happens between us."

"I don't know who I am anymore. I have to belong to myself before I can belong to anyone else."

He shifted his chair closer and draped an arm around her shoulders. It felt strong, comforting, and altogether right.

"I have to figure this out on my own." Her voice was harder than she'd intended.

The disappointment in his eyes hurt her, but she had no choice.

"You're the woman I want to be with, have children with, grow old with." He trailed his thumb along her cheek, then lowered his head.

She pulled away, knowing his slightest touch could destroy every shred of her resolve.

"I'm a simple man. I know what I want. What I want is you."

"You're anything but simple."

"Simple enough to know I'm sitting here with the woman I love and wasting an opportunity to kiss her." He paid their bill and cupped her elbow to draw her up and away from the cafe.

Ford was saying he loved her. She had no reason to doubt his word. What she doubted was her ability to return his feelings. How much of her mother was in her? And how much of Sam? Her heritage was shaky, as was her faith in herself.

She had to work through her emotions. Facing Ford's strength and energy made that impossible. He deserved a woman who knew who and what she was.

Unfortunately, she wasn't that woman. She had only to remember what her mother did, what Sam did, to know she might never be what he needed.

Tears blocked her view of him, but it didn't matter,

because all she could see was the future. A future without Ford.

He cupped her shoulders, bringing her close enough that she could smell the clean, male scent of him. She inhaled deeply and knew that this scent would be forever imprinted in her memory.

"Come with me. Make a life with me."

She gulped in a bracing breath and steeled herself against the disappointment in his eyes. She had hurt him, had hurt them both. She wanted to snatch back her earlier pronouncement, to say what he wanted to hear, to give them both that gift. And she knew that she couldn't.

Her heart leapt at the promise in his words, one that was echoed in his eyes.

She longed to do as he said. It would be so easy, so very easy, to give in to him.

Somehow she found the courage to push away from him. It cost her everything she had, and she trembled with the effort.

"You're afraid to reach for a future because of the past," Ford said, his voice November cold. "I never thought of you as a coward. Looks like I was wrong."

His words sank into her like razors of ice, chilling her heart even as they drew blood. The coldness pushed out all feelings of warmth and life from her.

His lips tightened. White lines fanned the corners of his eyes.

She ached to erase the grief from his face, his

heart. Because no words could banish the pain, she said nothing and stared into the bright bitterness in his eyes.

For endless moments they simply stared at each other bleakly, saying nothing, telegraphing what they felt, what they were afraid to feel, with only their eyes.

Ford stood mute and helpless against her plans. The right words were out there somewhere, if only he could find them—the words that would make her understand that they belonged together.

Disappointment settled his feet firmly on the ground. Every scent, every sound, became permanently etched in his memory. The smell of too-strong coffee from the cafe nearby, the fading light of the sun, the rasp of his own breathing.

"I love you." He spaced out the words to give her time to absorb them.

He wanted to take her into his arms. That should make everything simple, but he knew better. The wrong move on his part could send her running.

Still, to hold back took every ounce of self-control he had. *Kiss her. Pull her close. Let her know how much you want her, how much you need her.*

He was tempted, so much so that his muscles shook with the effort to keep his arms at his sides.

The silence stretched long and terrible between them.

"Everything I want is right here," she said at last.

"I don't need to go chasing all over the country for something I already have." More softly she added, "My roots are here."

She was right. Her roots *were* here. Why had he ever expected she would give that up for the little he could offer?

He turned and somehow managed to walk away from her. He knew if he looked back, no power on earth could make him leave.

Cady watched as he walked away, as if he didn't care one way or the other. She swallowed a sob. He asked too much. She bit down on the urge to call him back.

The pain was like a sore tooth she kept poking with her tongue. He hadn't lied to her, hadn't promised anything different than he was offering her now. She'd known he was going to leave. So why was she feeling so depressed?

With no heart for doing anything else in town, she went home but did not go inside.

Sunset in the Springs was nature at its best. The sun was riding low in the sky, all bleeding colors and fiery light. Heat still clung to the day, but she felt a bit of the evening cool.

She didn't question her decision to linger and absorb the panorama of land and sky. Life held little enough true beauty to waste even a moment of what stretched before her. The quiet was unbroken save for the gentle lowing of the cattle. Even that was soothing.

The drab gray of the plain changed to purple, the sky now a rose-red flush on which vermillion clouds rested, the distant peaks gleaming like rubies.

She was besieged by color, the richness and the thickness of it. The land and sky fairly vibrated with color—mauve and rose, violet and turquoise. She blinked, needing to rest her eyes for a moment from the brilliance that assailed her.

She continued her vigil on the porch, far past the time when dusk melted into the gray of twilight. Night came, relieved only by a sprinkling of stars.

The wail of a wolf, full-voiced, crying out the loneliness of the desert, sliced through the night. She listened and shuddered with the plea she heard in the cry, a plea that resounded in her own heart.

The wolf's howl was eerily melancholy and heart-breakingly wistful. Hunger throbbed in it—hunger for its mate, offspring, life.

The wolf howled again.

She couldn't help it. She shivered, whether from the plaintive sound or the cool night, she wasn't sure. Inevitably, her thoughts turned to Ford. A man had no right to make himself vital to a woman's exis-tence and then leave her.

She felt the ache start around her heart, then squeeze in. She locked her unhappiness away there.

Hot tears rimmed her eyes but didn't fall. They could not ease the throbbing ache in her heart. Only time could do that. Time and distance.

Lots of time. Lots of distance.

Morning found her still convinced that she had done the right thing, but it was scant comfort in view of the all-consuming loneliness that chilled her through and through.

She knew that. She also knew she couldn't do anything different when she was filled with so much doubt. Doubt about Sam, about herself, about everything she thought she knew.

How could she trust her instincts when she didn't know herself? She knew the facts of her life, but what of the woman inside? Everything she believed about Sam, about herself, had been put to a test.

She had to rebuild that belief and maybe, just maybe, find herself as well.

Before she met Ford, she'd thought she knew what loneliness felt like. Now she realized she hadn't had a clue.

Chapter Twelve

People like Ford McKinnon didn't dream. They planned. His whole life had been one long series of plans—sheriffing in small towns all over the Southwest until he'd earned the chance to be a United States marshal.

Why couldn't Cady understand that Colorado Springs couldn't hold the one dream he'd ever allowed himself?

For a moment he allowed himself to picture the two of them building a life together, he working as a marshal and Cady writing for the Denver paper. Eventually there'd be children. His heartbeat quickened at the idea of raising their child. He snapped his thoughts out of what-might-have-been and back into reality.

His humorless smile was a razorlike acceptance of the heartache of her refusal. What had he expected? Cady came with roots. Of course she would choose them over him.

He'd been a fool to think differently, to hope for a different outcome. Just because he didn't have any didn't mean that he didn't understand the importance of roots.

She wasn't a woman to leave . . . and he wasn't a man to stay.

He felt sick that he'd lost Cady, yet, at the same time, a curious relief took hold. Being alone was something he understood.

He gave the town council notice. No point in putting it off. With the mayor and other members of the council, Ford took a seat in the schoolhouse, straddling a chair.

"We need you," the mayor said after Ford had stated his intention to leave. "Sure, the rustling is over, but we have other problems. Problems you can solve. You've made a place for yourself here. You won't find us ungrateful if you decide to stay."

Flattered at the invitation, Ford hesitated. He could have Cady and a job he enjoyed. Then he thought of his goal, the goal that had seen him through the lonely years when he'd had little else to sustain him.

The mayor sweetened the pot with a raise in salary.

"I'm sorry." Ford stood. "My future isn't here." He shook hands with each of the men.

It was ironic, he thought, that he had found the woman with whom he could picture sharing his life, only to discover that her dream kept her planted where she was, while his dream took him away.

Lately he'd begun to realize the price he'd paid for his self-imposed isolation. He had grown accustomed to being alone. Lately, though, he'd started to feel lonely.

There was a difference, the difference being the moment you knew that you no longer liked being alone as well as you liked being with someone else. The right someone else. That's when being alone turned to loneliness.

Ford picked up the paper. A smile inched across his face as he read Cady's latest editorial. She didn't mince words about the political shenanigans at the state capitol.

She was making a name for herself. Her objective reporting of Sam's part in the rustling had earned her respect, both in the Springs and throughout the state. Those small-minded enough to criticize her for her father's mistake were in the minority.

He'd learned that her plans to sell the ranch had gone through. A middle-aged couple from Kansas had bought it. It was nice, he thought, being able to admire her as well as to love her.

Ford slammed a fist into his palm and groaned

aloud the name that haunted him. "Cady." No other woman, not even Margaret, had come close to taking root in his heart as Cady had.

Hurt, as unexpected as it was sharp, scraped at him as he remembered her reaction to his proposal, and he wondered if he'd misread her feelings all along.

He had plenty to do, more than enough to keep him busy from dawn to dusk, but he was having difficulty concentrating. His attention, as fleeting as a desert mirage, kept wandering. He didn't have to look far for the answer.

Cady.

He thought of her constantly, with the kind of longing that kept him up at night, took away even his need for solitude.

He remembered the softness of her hair, the feel of her lips under his, the touch of her hand. He ached to go to her, to take her into his arms and hold her.

His exasperation with her didn't diminish his admiration for her courage, her commitment to her beliefs, or her generous heart.

"Hey, Ford. You gonna stare into space all day?" Robb asked.

Ford gave a guilty start. He read the speculation in his deputy's eyes and knew that Robb was puzzled. Ford didn't blame him. Heck, he didn't understand himself these days.

He needed space. With scarcely a word to Robb,

he strode out of the office, saddled Hawk, and let the big gelding have his head. Hawk must have sensed Ford's mood, for he took off at a gallop, his powerful legs eating up the ground.

When Hawk slowed, Ford realized how hard he'd pushed both of them. He dismounted, patted the horse's neck, and walked him, letting them both cool down.

Autumn had crept up on the Springs, the seasonal changes subtle in the high country. Still, the air had a bite to it, the sky darkening earlier than it had a month ago.

Deer foraged closer to town, looking for food. They knocked down fences faster than the ranchers could repair them. He stood in the unrelenting wind and smelled hints of winter. The days had grown shorter, the nights longer. The damp of autumn clung to the ground, the evening eerily quiet.

The quiet split to the cry of a wolf. It rose—strange, wild, eerily mournful—not the howl of a predator but that of a lone creature, hungry for its mate. The cry echoed in his soul.

When the quiet came again, the silence was more terrible than the fierce baying of a moment before.

He and the wolf were brothers.

Wolves mated for life. When the mate died or was killed, the other remained alone. Lone wolf.

He laughed without humor.

Hawk whickered.

"Okay, fellow. Time to head home." Ford mounted and flicked the reins.

Nothing seemed right without Cady. A hundred times over the last week he'd told himself he was better off without her, but he couldn't make himself believe it because he knew it wasn't true.

He folded up his thoughts and headed to the cabin. An overwhelming sense of loneliness swept through him. Cold and hungry, he didn't have the energy to sort through his emotions. He tried not to think of Cady.

Of course, he thought of her.

She had taken away his contentment. Honesty forced him to admit that the fault was his, not hers.

He felt his aloneness all the way to the core. Not loneliness. He didn't long for company. He was alone in the truest sense of the word. He knew nothing about belonging and everything about being an outsider. For a few golden weeks, with Cady, he had forgotten.

At the barn, he wiped down Hawk, making sure the big gelding had fresh hay. He walked to the cabin, his boots stirring up dust. He kicked a clump of red clay out of the way, then looked for another chunk to kick. He didn't go inside but hunkered down on the rough step of the cabin.

Women. He'd already admitted he didn't under-stand them, but he'd thought he had known Cady. She'd shared her grief with him over Sam, then had chosen her work over him.

He braced against the expected pain. It slammed into him with undiminished power.

He directed his gaze in the direction of the town that had so quickly become home. *Home.* Where had that notion come from? Colorado Springs had never been anything more than a springboard to his next job. He'd put an end to the rustling. That should be enough.

Instead, all he could think of was a pretty newspaper woman with a feisty mouth and a quick mind. He recalled how she'd felt in his arms the night of the dance—exactly right, relaxed and trusting, as she leaned against him. He couldn't get the memory out of his head and realized he didn't want to. He wanted her in his head, in his heart, in his life.

He felt a squeezing around his heart, a sensation that had become so common since he'd met Cady that he was almost used to it.

The woman could outdo a mule in pure stubbornness, and still he wanted her. The ache around his heart loosened enough for him to slide into a smile.

He glanced at the sky. The clouds had hunkered down like a grumpy neighbor. They shrouded everything in a shadow of gloom, mirroring his mood.

He rubbed the stubble on his chin. He hadn't shaved that morning. Or the morning before that.

He'd rented this place when he moved to the Springs. The barn had looked as if it hadn't been painted in years. Rusty hinges had caused gates to creak; the doors had hung unevenly from rotting frames. Vermin had infested the hay supply. He'd worked every free hour to fix up the barn and was proud of what he'd achieved.

After stripping off his shirt, he picked up a pitchfork and mucked out the stalls. The push and pull of muscles felt good.

He wiped his hands on a rag and stood back to inspect the job. The stable smelled pleasantly of healthy and well-groomed horses. The stalls were clean, the hay fresh and sweet.

It was then he realized that all the work he'd done, turning a wreck of a barn into something he could be proud of, meant nothing. Doing something well didn't mean a thing if there was no one with whom to share it.

In the same way, putting an end to the rustling had brought satisfaction. But the satisfaction hadn't lasted.

He looked about once more at the place that had been his for such a short time. The farm had been a showplace at one time and could be again, if someone invested the time and the money in it.

Well, that someone wouldn't be him.

Cady dragged herself from bed by first light. The little sleep she had managed to get had not erased the pain that weighed upon her heart.

Early morning had long been a favorite time of

day for her, a time for reflection and thought. Now, though, it seemed unbearably lonely.

She stared out the kitchen window. The familiar sight of the mountains, looking close enough to touch, failed to bring her needed comfort. She let her gaze take in the farmhouse, barn, and acreage, remembering that it wouldn't be home much longer. When the new owners arrived, she'd move into the storage room behind the *Gazette* office.

Her sense of doom thickened. For what seemed the thousandth time, she told herself that ending her courtship with Ford was for the best. One thing was certain: She had to stay away from him. Her feelings for him made her too vulnerable.

She headed to town, to the *Gazette*. At least she still had that. Indian summer warmed the day. Not even the perfect autumn day, though, could drive away the darkness inside her. She carried it with her.

Emilie must have guessed that something more than Sam's part in the rustling was troubling Cady but was too tactful to say anything. "When you want to talk, I'm here."

Cady was grateful for her friend's understanding. She could not have faced questions or advice just now, however kindly meant.

She sank back into a chair and tried to still the pounding of her heart. How was she supposed to get through the rest of the day, much less the rest of her life?

Without Ford, she had no reason to do anything but work. Stinging tears gathered in her throat. Determinedly, she swallowed them back.

She learned that Cal Browne had left town. It seemed others shared her feelings about the man. She couldn't help wondering if Ford had something to do with Browne's decision to leave.

With Ford's help, Emilie had applied for and received a writ of divorce. The circuit court judge had approved it. In a few months she would be free to get on with her life.

Emilie had a new look of pride in her carriage, and she wore it well. She'd tried her wings and found she could fly. Cady was proud of her friend.

Ford made no attempt to get in touch with her. She was grateful for that. The sooner she put him out of her mind, the better. Sometimes, at work, she was actually able to succeed, and, for a short while, she was almost her old self. But at home the memories returned, so vibrant and alive that she could almost feel his arms around her, his lips touching hers. With those sensations came an anguish that tore at her heart.

The nights were the worst of all. She relived every moment they had spent together, savoring each precious memory and storing it up to take out and replay when the pain grew too great. Even the knowledge that she was only driving the knife deeper into her heart failed to stop her tormented thoughts.

Sleep did not come easily, if it came at all. And then her dreams were filled with Ford. Ford teasing her, Ford kissing her, Ford holding her as if he would never let her go.

Life hinged upon decisions, both large and small. Her decision to return to Colorado Springs after Sam's death had brought her both heartache and love.

She accepted both and knew they were part of the whole. When she thought of the future, she wondered what it would hold.

Her work took on new importance. The Denver paper had picked up her story. While she chafed under the idea of more people learning of Sam's part in the rustling, she couldn't deny the spurt of pleasure she felt at the attention her work had received. Nor would she turn away from the facts simply because the truth hurt.

Integrity and truth were the watchwords of her profession.

The telegraph made it possible to send stories to other papers and to receive stories from the outside world. State and national news made their way into the paper, and she took pride in its content.

Local merchants started inquiring about advertising space. For the first time since she'd started the paper, it was showing a respectable profit.

Her dream was coming true . . . and she was miserable. She reminded herself that she was fortunate to have her dream come true. Except she didn't feel lucky, only deprived and unbearably lonely.

Emilie cleared her throat, and Cady stirred herself enough to look at her friend. "You were a friend to me when I needed one. Let me be the same to you."

Cady dredged up a smile. Under Emilie's gentle prodding, she told the other woman what had happened.

"He's going to Denver and wants me to go with him. He asked me to marry him."

"What's the problem?"

"I don't know who I am anymore," Cady said, the words coming out in a hoarse whisper.

Emilie gave Cady a long look, as though trying to read her soul. "You're Cady Armstrong, the same as you've always been."

"I'm afraid I lost that Cady."

Emilie pressed her hand. "You haven't lost anything. Will you be all right?"

"No," Cady said honestly.

When Emilie had gone, leaving the office depressingly quiet, Cady tried to sort through what had happened.

Stop it, she told herself. *It's for the best.* Try as she would, though, she doubted she'd ever convince herself of that.

Getting Ford out of her mind was proving next to impossible. She threw herself into her work. Fortunately, the paper demanded her full concentration.

Heartache was no excuse for neglecting her work, and she had moped about for too long. With a vengeance, she threw herself into her weekly editorial, finding relief in the act of writing.

After an hour, Cady leaned back in her chair and reached around to gently knead the tense muscles in her shoulders and neck.

Light shone through the room's one window, sending fingers of sunshine across the walls. She watched the play of light and shadow, fascinated by the subtle shifts in color and patterns. She loved Ford, but she couldn't go with him. Tears spilled over and ran unheeded down her cheeks. She cried for herself, for Ford, for what might have been.

When she'd cried herself out, she acknowledged that she was so in love with him that she could barely think straight. *When it happens to you, it'll hit hard,* Sam had told her. As usual, he had been right.

She felt the familiar lump in her throat at the thought of Sam, but she was learning to deal with it by acknowledging the pain rather than ignoring it.

She was feeling better. She repeated that thought over and over in her mind, as if sheer repetition could make it true. The longing for Ford haunted her a little less frequently. The pain was a little less intense.

And the honest corner of her brain called her a liar.

The truth was, she was miserable. It had been the

longest week of her life. If you could call this living, she thought wryly. All the joy had vanished from her world, and, for the first time in her life, she dreaded getting up and facing each new day. Not even the intense grief she had experienced after Sam's death and upon learning of his involvement in the rustling equaled her total despair at the thought of losing Ford.

Images of him flickered through her mind. His sensitivity when she had learned of Sam's part in the rustling. The sense of humor that surfaced at odd moments. She feared she would always judge other men by him, and she was very much afraid that none would measure up.

She attempted to bury her pain in the ordinary tasks of writing and rewriting. She hoped that if she didn't have time to think, it might be possible to forget.

Unfortunately, that tactic didn't work any better than it had at Sam's death. Ford's absence from her life left a void that she feared nothing and no one would ever fill.

She pulled her shawl more closely around her. With a pang, she recalled that she'd worn the shawl to the Sweetheart Dance. Ford had placed it on her shoulders with touching gentleness.

If she went home, she'd have to deal with the memories and the loneliness. Another week and she would leave the farm for the final time.

The couple who had bought it sight unseen would be arriving then. The bank president had arranged the sale.

Sam had brought her up to have confidence in herself, in her abilities. The independence he had instilled in her had served her well. She had held on to that when she'd signed the papers that would pass the Armstrong farm to other hands.

She closed the *Gazette* office early but had no desire to return to the cabin. The house she had called home for so many years held no comfort. It was empty and lonely and sad. Instead, her footsteps took her to the cafe.

Heads turned in her direction, and she sensed the eyes on her, heard the expectant hush. Too late she realized that she'd arrived at noon, when the cafe drew men taking a break from work and women in town to do their shopping at the Mercantile.

Most of the furor over Sam's part in the rustling had died down, but gossip about her and Ford had spread hot and furious through Colorado Springs. She was too weary to resent it.

Other patrons gave her curious looks. Her ready smile and quick sense of humor were conspicuous by their absence. Her skin had lost its luster, and she'd grown noticeably thinner. Her clothes hung loosely on her.

She took a table, keeping her back turned to the

other patrons. She discovered she wasn't in the mood for company after all.

When Doris showed up with a cup of coffee, Cady kept her head down, not wanting to encourage conversation.

"Heard you and Ford had stopped stepping out together," Doris said as she refilled Cady's coffee cup. "Something happen between the two of you?"

Cady's hand trembled as she reached for the cup of coffee, and a pang of yearning twisted through her.

The older woman put a hand on Cady's shoulder. "You're feeling raw right now. Give it time."

Cady tried hard to work her lips into a smile. It felt like a lie. "Nothing happened." That, at least, was the truth.

At Doris' raised eyebrow, Cady felt compelled to add, "We decided we weren't right together."

"You looked mighty right to me. Too bad I can't say the same for you right now—you look lower than a snake's belly."

"I'm fine." The lie was so patently obvious that Cady felt her cheeks heat with color. "All right, I'm not fine. That doesn't mean I want the whole town butting into my business."

"Horsefeathers," Doris said, exasperation whipping around the edges of her voice. "You're part of the town. You got troubles, we all got troubles."

Cady snuffled back a humorless laugh. She knew

that Doris spoke only the truth, and for a moment she wondered why she wanted to remain in a town where everyone knew everyone else's business and felt they had a right to give advice.

Doris didn't take the hint. "The sheriff's a good man. He's as straight and true as they come. Just like you."

Doris was right. Ford *was* a good man.

"Do you love him?" Doris asked.

"Love isn't the only thing in the world." Cady tried to smile, but it got lost in the pain.

"There's too much misery in the time we spend on this old earth to turn away happiness. You get to be my age, you start to appreciate the joys in life, both big and small. And love is the biggest one of them all."

Doris gazed at Cady with bleak understanding. "You think I never knew love? Never cried my heart out over a man? There was a man. A long time ago. He asked me to marry him."

Despite her misery, Cady was curious enough to ask, "What happened?"

Doris pinched up her mouth as though the memory were a painful one. "I turned him down."

Cady waited, sensing there was more to the story.

Doris stared off into space. "I grew up in Philadelphia. My family had a big house, servants, social position. I thought I had everything, until I met a man.

A gold-miner. He was back East to raise money to expand his operation. My father was one of his investors." She refocused on Cady's face. "We fell in love. He asked me to go with him."

"Why didn't you?"

"My father was convinced he was a fortune hunter and forbade me to have anything to do with him. That nearly drove me into his arms."

"What stopped you?"

"I was afraid. Afraid of the unknown. Afraid of leaving my comfortable life." Doris gave a half laugh, ragged around the edges. "Funny. I ended up coming west after all. Alone."

"You never married?"

Doris shook her head. "I had my chance. I lost it. Now I have the cafe." She gestured around her. "It keeps me busy."

"Are you happy?"

Doris gave a wry smile that failed to blossom into real happiness. "I have the cafe. My work. My friends."

Neither woman missed that Doris hadn't answered the question. Neither commented on it.

Doris fixed Cady with an unswerving look. "You've got yourself some questions to answer. Does he make you happy? Do you love him? Does he love you? Can you picture your life without him?" She took Cady's hand and pressed it between her own work-roughened ones. "When you can answer those questions, you'll know what to do."

Having said her piece, she stood and patted Cady's shoulder. "I'll let you be. You'll be wanting to think on what I said."

Chapter Thirteen

Cady thought about her friend's words during the ride home. Strange that she should find the key to solving her problem there, in the cafe. She'd never suspected Doris of having had a great love.

She recalled Sam's saying that you never really knew someone, knew the hurts, both small and large, that went into making up that person.

As he'd been about so many other things, he'd been right about that. Steady, unflappable Doris, with an unending stream of gossip and common sense, had once loved a man so much that she'd never looked at another.

It was something, Cady reflected, to chew on. At the cabin, she sat and stared out the window. Maybe she'd build a fire, though it was only early afternoon, and enjoy the whicker of flames. The idea was unexpectedly appealing and comforting.

Still, she didn't move. Instead, she thought back over her conversation with Doris. She needed to ask herself the questions Doris had posed to her.

Did Ford make her happy? Most definitely.

Did she love him? Yes.

Did he love her? Yes.

Could she imagine her life without him? No.

She was in love with Ford McKinnon. Irrevocably, totally, in love with him. How had it happened so quickly? Yet love wasn't measured by the calendar. It came quietly, stealing up on one with a fine disregard for what should be.

She loved the simple goodness that had prompted him to help Emilie, a woman he didn't know but had promised to protect. Loved the wisdom he showed in dealing with a young boy. Loved the gentleness he used with his animals. She needed his arms around her, his lips upon hers, his strong presence.

With startling clarity she realized that one of the best ways to free herself from the shadows of the past was to accept the love she'd found with Ford.

This was what she'd been looking for without knowing it. This feeling of rightness, this sense of belonging.

Love.

She loved him. She loved the strength and the gentleness that surprised her each time he revealed them, a gentleness that was all the more potent because it was accompanied by strength.

It was time to move out of her state of mourning and rejoin life. She had her work and the sense of purpose it gave her, but without Ford, it would be only shades of gray. He put color into her life. Color and laughter and frustration and everything else that had been missing for the last week.

Running her own newspaper wasn't the biggest challenge of her life. Falling in love was bigger and infinitely more important.

Love.

It had blinded her. It could also let her see. She wasn't her mother, she thought, the familiar sadness only a gentle regret now. Or her father, Sam, who had tried to be both mother and father to her.

She was, Cady thought, herself.

The realization brought with it a heady sense of freedom. Why had she been so afraid? A wonderful, strong man had offered to share his life with her. She had turned it down because of fear, because of the past.

She recalled the way Ford had looked at that moment when he spoke his last, loving words to her. Now, she accepted them, embraced them. Love was too rare and precious a gift to reject because of uncertainty or fear of tomorrow.

Joy touched her spirit. She held on to it, or it held on to her. So full was her heart, she couldn't tell which. And she felt much of the rawness and pain of the past week ebbing away.

The wind spattered sand and pebbles against the windowpane, pulling her from her musings. She dismissed it as the normal gusts that blew over the Colorado prairie.

When the squall of the wind grew louder, though, she started outside, stopped, and stared at the sky.

Storm clouds—tall, dark, angry thunderheads—dimmed her view of the mountains. She'd seen that blackness before, years ago when she was eight.

Memories of the tornado that had ravaged the fledgling town returned with a vengeance. She remembered how the wind had left one side of the town intact but demolished the other.

The clouds moved on, leaving the sky as blank as a child's school slate. Oddly, the empty sky was more threatening than the cloud-laden one of moments before. The air had a still, flat quality to it.

She didn't try to talk herself out of her foreboding. Sam had taught her to trust her instincts. Those instincts were screaming that a storm was coming, a bad one.

She cupped a hand over her eyes and stared into the distance. There. To the east. A funnel cloud was moving in the direction of the farm, picking up speed with every second.

The animals came first. She freed the chickens, the horses, and two cows, knowing they'd find shelter.

Judging how much time she had, she tacked the shutters closed. Though the farm would soon belong to someone else, she would do what she could to protect it.   •

Just as she started to the cellar, the funnel touched down. A tornado. Sand filled the empty sky as the wind, a whirling dervish, spun her around.

She fell, hit her head on a loose board. The blow temporarily stunned her. She put a hand to her forehead, then brought it away to find blood. There was no time to worry over it.

The wind slapped at her, angry claws digging deeply. She raced against it, praying with every breath. The sour taste of fear coated her mouth. Doggedly, she kept moving. She scrabbled her way across the rough ground, grabbing hold of anything she could to anchor her.

The cellar was but a few feet away. Behind those double doors lay safety. She didn't take her eyes from them. Finally she grasped the doors and yanked them open. She fell into the dank darkness, the breath knocked from her, and prepared to wait out the tornado.

As the blackness closed around her, she hugged her knees, grateful to be alive. She promised herself that if she survived, she'd find Ford and tell him that she loved him.

She felt the last of her uncertainties about herself slipping away. Ford McKinnon was in her heart to stay. With the acceptance of that came an acceptance of her own future.

Something bad was in the air. Ford could feel it. It was more than the ominous hush, more than the hard look to the sky. He stared at the distant horizon, where the plains met the unbroken strip of dingy sky.

The back of his neck prickled. He'd learned not to ignore the sensation. It had saved his life more than once.

He had lived through a dust storm or two in his time, had even had the stuffing kicked out of him by a tornado when he'd done a stint as sheriff in western Kansas. He didn't care to relive either one.

He trusted his gut when it came to sensing changes in the weather. There were signs. Birds disappeared. Even more than the unnatural silence was the absence of clouds. The sky was gunmetal gray; no white puffs drifted lazily across it. The unrelenting flatness of it made the hairs on his neck stand at attention.

Odds were, whatever it was would give the Springs a pass and take out its fury farther east, where the earth flattened and stretched as far as the eye could see. Still, he didn't like the feel to the air. It had a foul taste to it. He scraped a palm over his chin, ruffling a day's worth of bristles.

In contrast to the earlier stillness, the air stirred, the wind soughed.

Ford cupped a hand over his eyes and stared into the distance. When he sighted the funnel cloud, he knew. *Tornado.* The very word had the power to cause panic. He'd seen it more than once, the unthinking terror when a tornado struck. People tended to run when they ought to stay put.

He had to act. He'd check the outlying farms first. If the funnel set down, they'd most likely be hit first. More than that, most of the farmers were inexperienced in weathering a storm. The soddies were scratching out a living on the unforgiving dirt and would risk their necks to save a pot or pan or some trinket rather than take shelter.

Tornados were erratic. Part of what made them so dangerous was their unpredictability. A tornado could take the roof off a barn and leave the rest of a farm untouched. Or it could wipe out a whole spread with capricious arrogance.

He'd witnessed the devastation firsthand. Though it had happened nearly ten years ago, he hadn't forgotten the sick feeling in his gut at the sight of a lifetime of work ravaged by a whim of nature.

In his travels, Ford had seen whole towns wiped out. He couldn't let that happen to his town. The words stuck in his mind. *His town.*

What had he been looking for when he came to Colorado Springs? He had told himself it was only another step in reaching his goal. He knew different now.

The Springs was his town. His home. In only a few short months it had claimed his heart and soul. Everything he'd ever wanted—even if he hadn't known he'd wanted it—was tied up in the town.

In the woman.

He wondered where Cady was, if she was safe. The agony of not knowing tore at him. At the moment, though, he was a sheriff first, a man second, and if the choice ripped the heart from him, it didn't matter. He couldn't let it matter.

His stride lengthened as his sense of urgency grew. He organized groups of men, delegating them to check on outlying farms.

"Don't go off half cocked," he warned. "Stay with your partner."

"You think it's going to hit us?" one of the men asked.

"I wish to heaven I knew," Ford answered. "But what I do know is that we can't afford to take chances.

"Free your livestock. They'll find their own shelter. Bring your families to town if there's time," he instructed. "There's safety in numbers."

He boarded up the sheriff's office, headed to the livery stable, and saddled Hawk. The empty sky had filled with dust clouds. Ford rode low in the saddle.

The wind nearly took his head off. He hunched lower and pushed his way through the stinging sand. His hat was tossed aside, the wind plastered his long coat against him, and still he forged ahead.

He checked on his assigned families, helped them secure their cabins as best they could, then instructed them to take shelter in their cellars.

The Henriksen spread was the last. He found Lars Henriksen attempting to board up his cabin with Sonny's help. The man didn't know one end of a hammer from another but struggled on valiantly.

Ford didn't have time to waste on manners, but he couldn't strip away a man's pride, especially in front of his son. "Lars, you and Sonny see to getting the livestock out, then get your family to the cellar. I'll finish here."

Lars gave a grateful nod.

Ford yanked away the man's flimsy efforts and nailed boards over the windows. The cabin was little more than a shack, but it was home to the family.

He fought his way through the wind to the patient Hawk. Before he could mount, one of the discarded boards zipped through the sky like a pebble shot from a sling, missing him by scant inches. Hawk reared, and Ford spent precious moments calming him.

At last he was free to go to Cady.

Let her be all right. He repeated the words in his mind, a silent prayer. He was not going to go another day without her. He'd make her understand that they belonged together.

He would love her until the day he died. And probably after that too.

He wasn't going to just fight to keep Cady. He was determined to win.

The wind had stopped. The silence was far from peaceful, though; it brought with it an eerie calm. The unnatural stillness to the air pebbled his skin with goose bumps. He didn't trust the quiet any more than he did the wind. It reminded him of a rattler, drawing back, considering, before it struck and spewed its venom.

As suddenly as it stopped, the wind started again, with a vengeance. The sand slapped his checks and scraped his neck like shards of ice.

He reached Cady's spread and said a silent prayer of gratitude that, except for a few loose boards, it appeared to have weathered the storm.

Cady would have holed up in the cellar. He banged on the plank doors. His future depended upon finding a way to convince her that he loved her, that he'd spend the rest of his life proving it to her.

The howl of the wind nearly obscured the rapping on the cellar doors. Cady groped her way through the darkness to unlatch them.

"Cady!" Ford's voice carried over the wail of the wind.

He wrapped hard arms around her, pulling her against the lean length of him. He lowered his head and covered her mouth with his.

The grayness of the last days vanished as she

came alive under his touch. Slivers of lovely anticipation stormed her senses.

The kiss stretched out.

"I prayed you'd make it here," she said, and she
held on to him. Her heart swelled. There was so
much she wanted to say.

He held her close, and she drew strength from his
nearness. Slowly, gently, he took her face in his hands
and kissed her again, a long, tender kiss that said
everything.

A brush of warmth. A promise of forever.

Her heart collapsed in her chest.

Love rippled through her, a sweet wave of longing
that flooded her heart.

"We're never going to be apart again," he promised.

"It's always going to be you, only you. I belong
wherever you are." Her eyes, luminous with unshed
tears, didn't waver from his. "I love you, Ford McK-
innon. Nothing's going to change that."

They climbed from the cellar, and Cady inhaled.
The air had the peppery taste of the aftermath of the
storm. The sun dipped in the west, reliable as ever, as
though the violence wreaked upon the land had never
happened.

It was a day for new beginnings and hope. She embraced both, a piercing quiver of excitement zinging
through her.

A hawk swooped over the prairie. Cattle mooed

plaintively. Nature had visited her fury upon the land, and it had survived. Pummeled and bruised, it had emerged stronger for the storm.

Just as she had.

It was a lesson she wouldn't soon forget. Survival wasn't a right. It was something you earned.

For the first twenty years of her life, Sam had taught her all he knew. She'd taken that, built upon it, and added a few lessons of her own.

Now she was taking the biggest step of all, adding yet another lesson to her life, that of trusting and loving a new man.

Ford planted his hands on her shoulders. "I love you. What are you going to do about it?"

"I'm going to love you right back."

"I want to make a life with you. Here in Colorado Springs. I've been thinking about buying the spread that I'm renting."

"It doesn't have to be here." She was beginning to understand that. "I can write anywhere. And I'll start another paper. In Denver."

"Everything I want is right here." Ford framed her face in his hands. "This is home. For both of us." He touched her face with one finger, swiping a tear from her cheek.

He dropped to one knee. "Cady Armstrong, will you marry me?" He reached into his pocket and produced a plain gold band. "I love you."

She could see it in his eyes, feel it within her own

heart. She was terrified and thrilled and everything in between of what was being offered. She pressed a hand to her chest, as though to push out air. She couldn't find any.

She told herself to breathe, but breathing seemed incidental to rejoicing.

She stared at her hand clasped in his, at the gold band shimmering under the Colorado sun, which now reappeared, nature's benediction after the violence of the tornado. "I love you." The words slipped out, as easy as a breath, as natural as a sigh.

A smile blossomed like a rose on her lips. His heart leapt, then stuttered at the love that shone from her eyes.

Their life together was bound to have bumps and rough patches. He looked forward to those as much as he did the quiet times. All were part of the whole.

"I love you."

Hearing the truth in her words, reading it in her eyes, he knew he had found what he'd been searching for. Love. A home.

A place to belong.